I0626538

Outlaws And Their Ballads

E.N. McMahon

Copyright © 2019 E. N. McMahon
All rights reserved.
Cover Art Copyright © 2019 Matt Smith
All rights reserved.
Published by Nick de Blegny Publishing
ISBN: 1-7332647-0-1
ISBN-13: 978-1-7332647-0-9

DEDICATION

As ever, to Kevin.

ACKNOWLEDGMENTS

This book could not have been written without the constant support and insight of Kevin Rattan. Thanks also to Philip Spitzer for believing in this book.

I

The eleven little brides of Christ were the first to hear it. They were in the Church of the Sacred Heart, waiting in the front pews for the moment they might file out and receive the body and blood of Christ for the first time. Perpetuée LaFarge was closest to the window, which was stained glass, and arched. The top pane was open against the day's heat, and slanted outwards high above her head: it depicted a Jesus with amber-colored hair and an almond-shaped face, stumbling under his cross. Years after the event, Perpetuée told me again about the morning on which she rushed down the church steps along with eighteen other First Communicants, the girls in white net veils and stiff broad petticoats, and the boys in starched ivory suits, towards a bullet-ridden Ford, to plunge their hands through the shattered glass, and let the still-warm blood of the town's slaughtered outlaws seep into their skin.

"Father Ducie had just consecrated the host. The bells rang, and a wave of incense rose through the air like mist off a field of clover. There was a rustle in the bushes just under the window. Father Ducie was raising the chalice high, and it sounded like a car had backfired, right outside."

Her left eye was sightless, and drifted in its socket, aimlessly, but in constrained circles, like a boat caught on its own mooring. At her throat, there hung a Maltese cross, and she twisted its chain around her finger as she spoke. I had not seen her in many years, but it was clear to me that, for the last several of them, the most steadfast of her companions had been the shadows that filled her house. When her housekeeper led me in and I first spoke, it was as if one of those shadows had taken voice, and she tilted her head back in momentary surprise. The room smelled of lilacs that had lingered past their prime. I had to remind her that we had been friends growing up, coloring maps in school ("The Extent of Napoleon's Empire in North America"), pondering which would be our signature cologne water: rose, or violet, or lily of the valley; and quarrelling over whether our wedding dresses should be tea-length or full to the floor; purest white, or a tinted ivory. At the revelation of our shared past, her head ceased its slight wavering, and went still; but in the end it hardly mattered. As with everyone else I encountered in town, the slaughter of the outlaws proved the natural and consuming centerpiece of our conversation.

No one could recall with certainty why a First Communion had been held on that day at all, on a Wednesday, and not a Sunday. Some say it was because a wedding had been scheduled that weekend, and a Communion followed by a wedding on the same day was asking for too great a visitation of grace in too short a time. My mother pointed out that the name saint of the parish priest fell on the Wednesday, and by performing the First Communion on the same day, people were spared the trouble of attending two receptions. By "people" she meant the parish priest himself, whose ambitions in the direction of a larger and richer parish, one with a working organ perhaps, and a sizeable rectory with soft carpets throughout, she had long suspected.

Some said it was because the Lt. Governor and his entourage would be passing through town that day, and a First Communion would provide him with the ideal opportunity to display his ambition within a setting of piety, as well as flatter Father Ducie's aspirations towards the world beyond Saint-Baptiste. Others maintained it was simply because the Church of the Sacred Heart was due to be painted that weekend. Father Ducie himself defended that view. He had been campaigning all spring to have the hallways of the church painted a restful pistachio green. For several weeks before, he'd taken to stashing around the vestry sample sheets of color, from a chalky magnolia white to a lustrous burnt sienna, and he drew them out, and pondered them in odd moments.

"The first one you think of, though, is usually right," he said, years later. "I'd seen a bowl of butter mints at one of the parish functions, and I knew in my heart that a pastel was the note to sound." He wiggled his fingers in the air as though rifling through that long-gone candy dish. Then he straightened his cassock across his knees, and shifted in his chair. The clock in the next room stirred thickly in the dusty air, and struck four o'clock.

"Now those kids would have fainted from the fumes, and got wet paint all over their new outfits. I could already imagine the mothers descending on me out by the rectory grotto. So I decided to throw tradition to the winds, and hold the Communion on a weekday."

That much was in character. I remember my mother decrying Father Ducie's predilection for red pasta sauce, and nothing but, at the parish's Easter week supper. For that holiday, my mother herself championed a solid roast, a honey-glazed ham, or a garlic-studded lamb. It was tradition. "I have nothing against spaghetti and meatballs," she said, ceasing her folding of the bed sheets to raise her hands and make the irrefutable point, "but to celebrate the Day of the Resurrection?"

Perpetuée claimed that Father Ducie had expected to

be called to New Orleans that Sunday, to co-celebrate a Mass with the archbishop. "He had bigger fish to fry, that Duce!" she said, using her customary name for him. She raised her right hand, palm held flat, in a fascist salute. "There's no idiot like an idiot priest. He should have rushed out of that church ahead of us, and blessed those forsaken outlaws himself. They were dying."

She'd been saying that last part for years, and people in town had long suspected Perpetuée LaFarge of having an axe to grind. It was rumored that her Uncle Roland, a silent fisherman with a gold front tooth and skinned browned by the sun to the color of a new cigar, had once enjoyed an acquaintanceship both discreet and warm with the mother of the outlaw woman. Indeed, both her uncle and the outlaw woman had a slight cast to their right eye - a similarity remarked upon when the first most wanted pictures appeared in the post office. Such commentary was at first offered as a rabble-rousing jest, meant to give rise to strong and witty denials. But in response, the uncle merely smiled from the shadowy corner of his accustomed seat at the Saint-Baptiste café. His tooth gleamed in the murky light. He took a sip of his double-roast coffee, and shuffled the deck of cards a second time; and so people wondered if the jibe were true.

No one disputed that early in their career, the outlaws had robbed the gas station that one of Perpetuée's cousins ran on the outskirts of the parish. That double connection to the criminals, one substantiated and one speculative, rippled through her heart, and gave it a dark vein she savored in secret, like a fudge whirl that runs melting and hidden within a rockhard tub of vanilla ice cream. "That outlaw gal was just a little bit of a thing. Fingernails no bigger than a doll's. And that fellow Lloyd, when he saw my cousin was wearing shoes so old that the soles were taped on, why, he grinned, tossed Lounie a silver dollar, and drove off. Just like that." By that point in our conversation, Perpetuée's face had listed so far to one side

4

that her eyes were now aimed towards the doorway. She smiled at the memory, which seemed to be a spot that floated somewhere above the lintel. "And he did have such wonderful teeth."

Théramène Camus, the local dentist, attested to that fact too. Lloyd Cannon had been one of his first patients, when Théramène had no actual training in dentistry, but only the ambition in that direction. "He had an ulcer by his right upper molar, and it was giving him some pain. But for someone on the run, he took good care of those teeth. Told me it came from rinsing his mouth out and spitting over the state line every time they were chased out of town, and that sure happened often enough. He was sat in the shoeshine stand, his mouth wide open for me, and I was laughing and had to put the toothpick aside to keep from poking a hole through his gum. How was I to know the day after I drained that ulcer he would drive 300 miles and shoot down his first policeman?" He shrugged and looked out his office window drawn momentarily back towards the event I was attempting to re-imagine and have fall into place once more. "Perhaps if his toothache had gone on, they wouldn't have gone out that day and killed a man," Théramène said. "Or perhaps the pain would have driven him mad, and he would have killed so many more. A dentist is seldom called upon to make such judgements."

Théramène knew full well the pain of rendering an opinion outside his exact field of expertise. The same year that the outlaws were gunned down, his revisionist monograph on the founding of Saint-Baptiste had appeared in the history journal of the state university. And by the next issue, Théramène had heaped upon him the scorn and ridicule that professional historians reserve not for the villains of which they write, but for the amateurs who presume to jostle alongside them. "You'd think I was the one who executed that portugee slave in the town square," Théramène said, shaking his head. "All I did was bring the truth to light, and perhaps make use of a few alternative spellings along the way."

Théramène's father was a doctor, and his mother, a schoolteacher. She brought to the marriage not a serviceable dowry of china and silverware and tatting-work tablecloths, like the other women in town, but a convent education. With painstakingly erect carriage, she bore the headful of notions gleaned from her years at the Rosary Academy. All her children were named, insistently, after characters from the tragedies of Jean Racine: Théramène, Andromaque, Thésée, Mithridate, Iphigénie, and Athalie. The summer she was to be married, she had rescued a collected edition of the poet's works from the flooded basement of her parents' house. She fished the water-logged volume out by its binding with a two-pronged barbecue fork, Théramène once told me, and as she drew the soggy pages to her bosom, she looked skyward, and accepted them as an omen. The names sat absurdly on her children like antique coats from a costume box, warding off the conventions of the neighborhood, calling out its ridicule, and faintly smelling of the stagnant water from which they had been resurrected.

Perpetuée and I were in the same class as Théramène's sister Iphigénie. She labored under that name. It was at least as burdensome as the dark single brow that she carried across her forehead and gave her the eternal appearance of a squint. She was skittish of her father, and hung her head to one side around him as if half-expecting a blow, or an order to be sacrificed to appease the prevailing winds. She hid her lunch in the pockets of her school dress, and by noontime a circle of grease seeped through the front. She ate alone and in secret, sneaking away into the cloakroom, and sat amidst its shadows, glancing about and cringing as if she feared her classmates would happen upon her in the act of consuming a fried egg sandwich.

Even before the guns fired into the car that shone in the May sunlight with the color of the desert sands,

Iphigénie claimed to have met the outlaws herself, out in a sugar cane field one Saturday morning in February. It was cold and the wind blew, near straight up and down, like to husk the earth of everything on it, but oh they were nice to her, she'd say, and a sigh ran through her thin body like a shiver.

"They promised to buy me an ice cream and a box of crackerjack on top if only I would smile. And I did, a little, but then the man said aw shucks, the superette was too far to go, so the lady she gave me the last of her tube of lipstick, and said didn't I look a princess. Then she put her hat on me, flat as a lozenge and the color of a sarsaparilla drop, and she said looky here, Lloyd, shouldn't this gal ought to be in pictures? And he looked up from the hood of his car where he'd been working, and he said, you know, I surely ought to." At the memory, whether one week old, or thirty-odd years, Iphigénie braved the weight of her brow, and raised her nose a little higher.

Her older sister, Andromaque, snorted the first time she heard the story. She was peeling an unripe apricot, and, with one eyebrow cocked, she was ready to make a remark as tart as the fruit. Iphigénie got up from the porch step where she'd been sitting beside me, and ran around the side of the house, led by her jutted-out chin, and trailed by her shadow, and the dangling belt of her school uniform. "That Lloyd looks pretty good in pictures himself," Andromaque called out after her, "especially the most wanted variety."

It wasn't clear why the outlaws had been driving in the vicinity of the Church of the Sacred Heart at the time of the mid-week First Communion. The church was well off the main road, set just a few streets in from the sluggish, flea-infested backwater. When it had been built forty years before, the Church of Sacred Heart had been envisioned as the jewel in the crown of a thriving seafront with prosperous marinas, busy fishing piers, and a cannery employing over a hundred workers. The twin square steeples of the church were to rise amidst the town's commercial district, and bestow grace, and a sense of scale. But some time around Sacred Heart's fifteenth anniversary, an oil tanker capsized two miles offshore. The water turned black and brackish. It teemed with dead fish; then it went bereft of fish altogether. And so, the Church of the Sacred Heart stood no longer upon the promised maritime-facing thoroughfare, but on a backroad that was ill-paved, and difficult for cars, when they came in, to negotiate. Indeed, some, including my father, wondered if Lloyd Cannon had headed down that road simply to demonstrate his prowess at the wheel, and the man had been done in by pride. Everybody, it seemed, ascribed a different rationale. Perpetuée told me that she believed the outlaws were through with their life of crime, and positively hungered to hear the saying of the true Mass. "They had not been practicing Catholics," she said, raising her finger into the failing light of her front room, "but perhaps in the end they become so."

Théramène maintained, with no good evidence but the legendary stupidity said to lurk in Lloyd's baby-blue eyes, that the outlaws had lost their way, and believed themselves to be heading on the main road for the west of Texas when the police opened fire on them and reduced them to a pile of rags. "They died happy," he told me years later, as he measured up a dose of Novocain, and shot it straight into his patient's lower right gum. Andromaque said from the beginning they were up to no good, but not fools, and they'd chosen a backroad to avoid the police and the federal marshals they knew were rapidly assembling against them. Iphigénie was convinced from the first they had come by the church to wish her well on her First Communion. She cited the china figurine of a ballerina that was found wrapped up in the back of the car as proof. The figurine had a lavender tutu, and a brown-ish bump of a hairstyle set over either ear, though by the time anyone in town saw it, the left clump had been chipped off by a stray shot. "The dancer even looked like me," Iphigénie said wistfully. "She always did say purple tones suited me to a T."

Others said Lloyd was driving down that peculiar route, to their deaths as it turned out, because the woman was determined to see her mother one last time, and Lloyd always gave her whatever she wanted. The woman was baptized Camille-Clotilde Roux, but she was always called Cammie. Father Ducie eventually mused that her troubles began with a name that in terms of saints, referred first to a hermit, and second, to the patron of exiles and unsatisfactory children.

"Perhaps that was an augur of what was to come," Father Ducie said years later, at a celebration of the Feast of Saint John. My mother passed him a plate of melting moments, and pointed out that the historical Clotilde had at least managed to tame a bloodthirsty leader, her husband King Clovis. "Would that auger had been borne out completely," my mother remarked. Confronted with such an indisputable, and possibly inexhaustible stockpile of obscure knowledge, Father Ducie took a cookie and went silent. A shadow passed over his face as if he was being walled up, brick by brick, alive.

Mrs. Roux's husband had died the year Cammie was born, carried off by an illness that varied with whoever was doing the recollecting: heart murmur, kidney trouble, black lung. The accounts agreed only as to the outcome. Cammie and her mother lived on the east side of town, in a district so outlying as to be almost within the Anglo section, beyond which only the Negroes lived. This location alone meant that while Cammie was one of us, she was already apart from us, for nearly everyone else in her neighborhood was Baptist, and attended services at a spare, flat-roofed building wedged in beside a gas station. On Sunday, their hymns and shouts resounded down the empty street, which was closed to business, but still smelled faintly of diesel and burnt rubber.

My mother had no quarrel with the Baptists, but she could not help pointing out that their churches were led by amateurs in plain clothes, who spoke in tongues, and played the guitar. Their neighborhoods were crisscrossed with scrabbly dirt yards, skinny yellow hounds who roamed at will, and tumbledown fences which reminded me of Mrs. Roux herself, with her hemlines falling loose. Nights other than Sunday, if you passed through those lost Anglo streets, you heard another kind of music, nasal and slow and lingering. You'd be headed down a road gone lavender in the night, and one of their songs would reach your ears, with a twang and quiver, a cowboy's lament that had got blown clear off the prairie, and carried like a stray bit of tumbleweed, to a town on the edge of a deadened sea.

In those months that her daughter was first making a name for herself, and our town, in banner headlines across the land, Mrs. Roux's face began to look as if it was turning inside out. Her bones rose sharply through her thin, bloodless-looking skin. She ran a ramshackle chicken farm, and every Tuesday morning she could be seen at LaFarge's superette, delivering a few dozen eggs. She hovered at the front entrance with the lingering presence of a ghost, smiling and nodding at nothing in particular as if she was trying to ward off unkind words before they could even take shape in a speaker's mind. Her eyes were as vacant as the windows of a deserted house, and I imagined there were long white spaces between her thoughts. My mother said she most likely lived on coca-cola and snuff. Her hair was limp, and her dresses were faded, and the most definite thing about her were the men's brogues she wore. They planted themselves at the end of her legs like exclamation points on a sentence that was so unremarkable it did not rightly call for any. She seldom spoke, and she never entered into controversy. In the aftermath of the slaughter, Mrs. Roux voiced no opinion as to why Lloyd Cannon and her daughter happened to be driving by a church on a backroad that morning in May.

Alongside that question, there was arose another, related one, and it plagued the people of the town for years afterwards, though they seldom gave voice to it. To some, it was altogether too rarefied a matter to bring up in the proximity to such obvious and actual bloodshed; to others, it was too sacred a mystery to be discussed alongside a tabloid story. But on either side, people disagreed as to whether or not any of the communicants had actually received First Communion on that day.

"I can still taste it today, the uncooked flour," Perpetuée said. "A dried-out little wafer. Only after the last of us had stood in line, opened his mouth and said 'Amen,' would anyone have dared to open the door of the church."

"Nonsense," her neighbor Josephina Rabideau said. "The doors would have been open the entire ceremony because the heat was so great. And the uncooked flour she remembers was the taste of that celebration cake her mother had baked the night before. She was not a gifted baker, that Mrs. LaFarge. Her hands were as heavy as two red bricks." Josephina felt such clumsiness keenly: she was tall and sparely-built, and austerely correct in all things, as befit her dancer's carriage, which was just short of haughty, like a deposed monarch's. On the most sweltering day of the year, the brim of her sun hat would be set at dead level with the horizon, and it never wavered. At a shop owner's greeting that struck her as overly forward, she would suck in her lower lip in disapproval, and the perpetrator felt justly castigated, and bowed his head in shame. In old age, she was as unadorned and serene as a novice nun, though she had scorned religious observance for as long as anyone could remember. So fine and so severe was her understanding of etiquette that it was rumored she had spent her first youth as a prostitute in the most exclusive bordello in New Orleans, as upright and sternly graceful as a candle flame bowing and flickering amid the red velvet, cut glass, and gilt.

When the shots first rang out, few people at first knew that anything out of the ordinary had happened. Josephina was running a dance class for the fourteen-year-olds in her studio a few streets over. It was on the top floor of an abandoned hat factory, the tallest structure in town, save for the church itself. Conflicting as it did with the oddly scheduled First Communion, the class was sparsely attended. Josephina had just put on a record of *The Merry Widow Waltz*. The reverberations of what turned out to be gunshot were so extreme that the needle wobbled like a high heel stuck between cobblestones. Upon the disruption of the three-quarter time, Antoine Beausoleil took the opportunity to drop from his arms the shoulders of Gabrielle Sante.

"She was always too fat," Antoine said, "and on that day she positively reeked of rose perfume." It was a smell that, since the wake of his grandmother the January before, reminded him of death.

"It was jasmine, not rose. I would never have been so obvious," Gabrielle said. "Rose is suitable for only old ladies and corpses. Even at the age of twelve I knew that much." A whitish cloud of talc rose from her ample bosom as she spoke, over three decades after the event. She ran a small flower shop located on the same block as the church, and lived alone above it. Much of her business was tied up with the Church of the Sacred Heart: weddings and funerals and feast days. By then, the buildings that lined the downtown streets were boarded up, and the grandest homes carved into rooming houses which sat sagging and half-vacant. Years before, Gabrielle's aunt, a spinster with no natural eyebrows, and a deep contralto voice incongruous from such a slight frame, had managed the florist shop. It was she who'd supplied the flowers for that First Communion: baskets of blue hydrangeas around the altar, and pots of lilacs filled out with ferns, and on the first ten pair of pews, bouquets of marguerites and baby's breath bound with yellow satin ribbon.

"Of course you know who the affair was really about, don't you?" Gabrielle said, that afternoon thirty-four years after the event. She plucked a chocolate from a silver dish, and dropped it into her mouth. She took her time, letting the chocolate melt down to the fondant, and continued. "Not the outlaws. They were well beyond the reach of ruin. Not the girl's mother either, or her father, whoever he was. I'll tell you - it was the one who set them up. Didn't you ever wonder who was waiting there by the church when it all happened? Lurking in the shadow of that giant cypress? His face bleached white and shaped like a cat's, pulling into a triangle no matter side you looked at it from – and then never seen again? I am not proud to be saying it." Her chin rose, and her back straightened. "My brother Louis." It was as if she had flung something of value and luster upon the table with that pronouncement, and we both sat back a moment, impressed, and considered its worth, and the way in which it caught the light.

But Louis's precise involvement was a matter of dispute as great as any other, except for the simple fact, that was less simple the more you inquired into it, that one Wednesday in late spring, by a whispering hedge of sweet mock-orange in full bloom, two outlaws in love and their Ford car the color of shimmering desert sands were riddled with bullets on the road outside the Church of Sacred Heart at the moment the host was consecrated.

I ought to have been in the church that day, but I was sick in bed when the shots were fired. Sometime in the course of that morning, not long before the outlaws would have been killed, I wandered down to the backyard of our house. My mother was sweeping the kitchen floor, and from the window, she glimpsed me in the corner of her eye. I dragged a lawn chair to the hedge, which carried a fringe of dewdrops along its dark, waxy green leaves. I climbed on top of the chair, and looked out towards the church. My mother went on sweeping. She was convinced I was jealous of the First Communicants, and she thought watching would be good for me, for through it, my soul would taste denial. Christ's body and blood could wait, she remembered thinking, for a proper ceremony that took place on a Sunday; and she swept the back hall with renewed vigor.

Though she was not in proximity of the church herself, she was among the first who knew what had happened, and more than that, who had been where when it did, and who had known what was being planned. As long as I can remember, knowing things had been my mother's characteristic role. She was the one the women of the neighborhood called upon for advice on shortening a skirt that ended in a flounce, or for baking a lattice-topped lemon tart that did not leak along the edge; and besides such tasks, ascertaining whether the priest in the next parish really had a sister who tried to jump off the roof of Woolworth's and was in the madhouse at Port-Richard; and if Mary Queen of Scots was truly, or only spuriously, implicated in the death of her first husband. Details emerged from her like items she had prudently stocked away in the pantry, like the dusty souvenir jar of Florida fig jam we were given one Christmas, and never opened.

At the moment the shots rang out and the town was marked with the blood of the outlaws, my father was in the shadow of a sweet mock-orange hedge, conversing with Lucien Poirier the baker about key problems of fatherhood. It was not "the" mock-orange hedge, the one that soon passed into town legend, and gave cover to the armed agents of justice, but another, insignificant one, on the far side of the post office, that had swallowed up a picket fence whole.

Poirier had just delivered another batch of cakes to the church for the First Communion reception, and his apron was stained with blue icing. During the night, a note had been slipped under his door. It was from Charpantier the sheriff, and directed Poirier to pipe a greeting to the Lt. Governor, who was passing through the town, onto the most imposing of the cakes. "Make sure it stands out," the sheriff's note said, and it went on to remind him that the Lt. Governor favored dark sunglasses on public occasions, and would only see the lettering if it was large enough, and presented in high contrast.

The strain was heavy upon Poirier, up since dawn, fulfilling the political obligations of others. He was obliged to mix some icing a deeper, unnatural blue; and his mouth wobbled as he recounted an unrelated woe that had contributed to his weary mood of dispirit. His ten-year-old son, a happy-go-lucky boy who was often glimpsed wandering around town with a shoelace trailing and his mouth hanging open, had failed his multiplication test for the fourth time: he announced, with Father Ducie there at the dinner table, that it made no never-mind since he was planning to become a daredevil rodeo star anyway. As Poirier spoke, my father shook his head in sympathy.

"All the while," he told my mother, "I was thinking the icing spattered on his apron looked like arterial blood, but when he finished talking, I told him that if he thought his son was a worry, I'd just seen Sante's boy, Louis, lurking around the backwater, counting on his fingers it looked like, and him at least sixteen - when the gunfire rang out, and I fell silent."

When the shots punctured the May morning, my father and Poirier were led by the sound of the gunfire to the Church of the Sacred Heart. A crowd had already gathered, and stood viewing the spectacle of pierced flesh, shattered bones, and flowing blood. "I had never seen anything like it," my father said, "except in a religious painting."

"Ain't nothing to look at, folks," Sheriff Charpantier told the crowd.

He may have attempted to smile, and according to

most accounts, he swept off his sheriff's hat at that moment. He was standing in front of the Ford sedan the color of desert sands, which had evidently rolled into a live oak by the side of the road, and was stuck there, the motor still running.

Some said the smell of wild garlic was thick in the air; others said the smell was definitely of lilac and gunsmoke and something metallic and thin and sickly that turned out to be blood. For his own part, my father said the smell of gasoline was so sharp it hit him in the gut like a hunger pang, and he almost threw up. Charpantier's fleshy pinkish face gleamed with a fine sweat. Then it was hidden from view, for the crowd was upon him.

II

The gaze of Lloyd's blue-green eyes was as bracing as a slap of a good aftershave. That's what Cammie Roux said out loud, one day in class when a thunderstorm had struck, and vast sheets of rain were lashing down upon the school's tall gray windowpanes. My older sister Jeanne-Patrice heard her, and Jeanne-Patrice was so dull she never lied, though how Cammie would have known about slaps of aftershave was anybody's guess. The weeks before she took to the road, in the year prior to the one in which her blood was splattered over the hedges outside the Church of the Sacred Heart, Cammie was sighted more than once lingering over the men's cologne display at Favereau's drugstore. She inhaled deeply of each bottle, in succession, and sighed.

Théramène had seen her there one day. Fénelon Favereau was heading down the aisle to unpack a carton of cold cream, and he brushed by Cammie Roux on his way. He made to ask her, as he passed, if she was casting about for a gift for her daddy, but recognizing her, he caught himself on the impropriety of the question. He changed it to "boyfriend," realized that was even more awkward, began to say "husband," then stopped mid-syllable, the word hanging off his lips like an exploding trick cigar.

"No, sir," she said, "I am enjoying the fragrance sensation for myself, if you don't mind." She was careful and awkward and charming in her way of speaking, Théramène said, and it reminded him of his sister Andromaque, when she was first learning to walk in high heels, and went teetering down their momma's front hallway. She had never seen the Pacific Ocean, Cammie said, but she imagined it would be the exact aquaish tint of Homme Virtu. But how a bottle of shaving water does cost, she exclaimed, and clapped her tiny hands together. (Théramène would have moved in for a closer look at this point, he recalled, and wished her good morning, but a shipment of canned peas was blocking the way.)

You got to figure, though, the smell comes free with it, the drugstore owner replied. He heehawed, nervously, and without mirth.

From her first year in catechism class, Cammie had been hearing about the tree of knowledge, and from near the beginning, you could imagine it had sounded good to her, something to look forward to, but not for too long, like luscious low-hanging fruit on a dry and dusty day. As she grew, she looked about her and saw there weren't one, but ever so many of those trees.

I remember seeing her, one Saturday morning, the winter before she was to take to the road. She was with a friend by the lipstick display in the drugstore, where she often went to daydream, and cultivate her desires. She was trying out each lipstick sample on offer. She was talking away, and her voice carried, with a light, insolent freshness. Straight down the line, every shade reminded her, precisely, of something she liked: blackberries staining your mouth on an August afternoon; the pink velvet that jewelry boxes from Peterson's were lined in; or a wild cherry ice so dark it looked like a scoopful of frozen chocolate. When I saw her around town in that year, I would linger at a distance, in the shadows, or at an aside, and watch. I wished she had been my sister. I wanted to be like her when I grew up, have her laugh, her succession of dresses bright as butterfly wings, and thin as slips, and her trail of men and boys.

The year Cammie was to take to the roads, and lend distinction to the town, was the same year Jeanne-Patrice assembled her Marian Medal project. After dinner, I watched as Jeanne-Patrice carefully cut out heavy, gold-edged illustrations of Our Lady, and pasted them on colored construction paper. Then, in pages of slanting, even script that was as impervious to the traffic of human life as a steady rain, she answered questions on the life of the Mother of God. One entry began, "Her life is a sacred mystery." In retrospect, it became clear to me that Cammie's was a profane one.

My news of her was mostly happenstance and incidental, even after she had been riddled with bullets by the Church of the Sacred Heart. I pictured her life in the town in a kind of tableau, like scenes from a movie strung along the bottom of its poster at the Bijou: Cammie at the five and dime, trying out a new powder compact; walking home from school through the dogwoods with some boy trailing after her; answering up in school, to the amazement of her classmates, and consternation of a Sister of St Joseph. What advertising illustrations promised, she already was. When she drank a bottle of coca-cola, she could make you feel the beauty of conceiving a thirst, nurturing it to its full, and quenching it at last. She had only to step up to a counter at a five and dime and finger an item, to make you feel the thrill of expenditure, and the means by which a product became a name-brand, and a shop good become one shared. Cammie Roux has got a purchase on life, my mother said once; and I duly pocketed the phrase. Around Cammie, the simplest transaction did become a kind of poetry, and commerce its own communion; and Cammie was both its inspiration and its patron. Without girls like her, there would be no ephemera, the stuff through which time brings itself to bear, and from which, most life is made.

She was the same age as my sister Jeanne-Patrice, a sad and abstracted creature who was in command of every geometric proof, but had no luck with the hair-iron. Those tonsorial failures were Jeanne-Patrice's outstanding physical attribute, and they highlighted the social affliction of her academic success the way a stigmata bears witness to its possessor's saintliness. In my mind, I can still see her, walking to school alone, skittish, aloof from her fellows, her dark hair stiffened into an arc that swung just above her white collar, and was always already flagging a bit. When Jeanne-Patrice came home with the occasional tale to tell about Cammie, it was as if she had been confronted with a rare and exotic bird let loose in the classroom, the very memory of its soaring wings still threatening to disarrange her unyielding and lamentable hair. She observed Cammie at close range, but through a cloudy and cracked disposition, and she never, to my recollection, had a single conversation with the girl.

After Cammie had been blasted to bits outside the Church of the Sacred Heart, several classmates came forth and confirmed that she had been a good student – though, as Sister Nanita's school report noted, "instinctive rather than methodical in her approach." She had insight but it was untrained; she blurted things out that made sense, but it was the kind of sense we accept if encountered in a dream, and smirk at if introduced into our waking hours. Once, the class was studying the climate of the Great Plains: its restless and billowing green springs, blazing hot summers, and winters stripped down and bare as gunmetal. Cammie was asked to name six Midwestern states, but she had been daydreaming and had no idea of the lesson. Sister Nanita read the passage out to her again, emphasizing, like a bad poet giving a public reading of his own verse, the billowing, the blazing and the stripping down. Then she asked Cammie if she could kindly identify the subject just described. Cammie paused a moment.

"The career of human passion," she replied.

According to Jeanne-Patrice, her classmates had been snickering up to that point, and preparing, with glances and shufflings of feet under their desk, to laugh out loud. But Cammie's response was so unexpected that no one dared laugh, and Sister Nanita rapped on her desk for order needlessly.

Moreover, the map of the United States, which could be drawn up and down over the blackboard like a small window shade, refused to retract after the geography lesson. To her annoyance, Sister Nanita was not only constrained from using the better part of the blackboard for the rest of the day, but confronted with the geographic icon of Cammie's brazen insouciance as well.

My mother concluded that Cammie was never innocent because, even afterwards (if she had had a real afterwards), she would never have understood the idea of guilty. Just after the story of the geography lesson had come home with Jeanne-Patrice, my mother observed, in Father Ducie's presence, that a girl like Cammie cuts her morals the same as dresses: on the bias, with plenty of give, and possessed of a flattering drape. Original sin passed her by, my mother went on, a girl like Cammie has to go out and make up ones of her own. Father Ducie coughed, rose halfway, and sat himself down a second time. Then he asked if another slice of lemon in his iced tea might not be too much trouble.

And when Cammie lay with Lloyd that first time, under a cypress doubtless touched silver by the lights of the occasional car passing by to destinations unknown, I liked to believe it was not simply physical intimacy that passed between them; or to be more accurate, for a girl like Cammie, intimacy was never simply physical. For as he lay his body over hers, and lay claim to her, she was laying claim him, to all the things he knew, and people he'd met, and places he'd been, that she had not: how to rig a suspension system into a Remington 20 gauge from an inner tube of a '31 Ford; the sound a saxophone solo makes, stirring up the shadows from the dance floor, the air kind of blowsy and hot, and spinning them around so fine that they finally made you shiver; the warden in Huntsville who could be bribed with the punchline to a joke; and the pretty little diner in Jamiston that had the best blueberry cobbler like his momma never did make. Plus, he had a car.

So she had him, and all those things he had spoken of and boasted about; and beyond them, that vast continent of things he had known and done but not even breathed a word of, became hers too. She never had to wonder why it was called the tree of knowledge; and she never imagined the bliss that was not knowing until she felt the pain of knowing; and both were called into being, and mingled, and separated, that night, and at the same moment. Then Lloyd buttoned up his fly, lit a cigarette, and said Joplin was fine pickings, but you couldn't beat Bienville Parish, least of all for the red beans and rice. And, she told her mother, she sat up in that bluish dark, and heard the crickets strumming in the fields, and smelled the diesel off a lumber truck laboring into the beyond. She felt that her world had expanded, and that everything was now in its proper place, floating there waiting for her to take each one up and transform it, like household items in a dream, or a Disney cartoon.

Louis, by contrast, seemed not to have left a single trace upon her. On his wedding night, his daddy had arrived at the threshold of the hotel, accompanied by the law in the form of Sheriff Charpantier; but she had already fled. When his daddy looked about him, and saw, he grinned, and so did Charpantier, who slapped his wide pink hand across the bed, which was still made up, and said, boy, you are bound to remain pure despite your best efforts.

I weren't man enough to keep her, Louis said. His eyes

watered mightily, and he went back to his slice of peach pie, but it might as well have been a wedge of glue, Gabrielle told me one afternoon thirty-four years later. She also said she could not help wondering exactly when and how his lackings proved too much for Cammie. Did it emerge in the course of the elopement that he did not know, say, Tahiti was an island; or did he fumble with the change at the ticket office, or assert himself stupidly with a waiter at dinner and then have to back down? She was his sister, Gabrielle said, but sooner or later, everyone who knew Louis had to join hands with him and confront the fact of his deep and incontrovertible lack. Maybe Cammie wasn't up to that kind of handholding, I said; but Gabrielle had just noticed Mrs. Charpantier passing by on the street in a dress of magenta and yellow plaid, and she was distracted.

The only thing Cammie left Louis was her bouquet of orange blossoms and white tuberoses. She had set it in the hotel bathtub because she thought the combination of flowers and running waters would seem like Hawaii, which she had seen in an old National Geographic. The smell of the flowers rose with the steam, then they wilted. Charpantier entered the bathroom, trailed by Louis, and snapped a few of the rose-heads into the water. He came back into the bedroom humming, and under the yellow lamplight, Louis hung his head in shame. When Gabrielle told me how it happened, I pictured Louis's shadow on the wall, and it was the truest portrait anyone could ever do of him, for it was as if his entire being had slipped into silhouette.

As a bride of one night, Cammie had been pretty; but as an outcast from matrimony, she came to positively glow. Louis's despair worsened. His face went from white to green, and his chin became more thin and pointy. The marriage was never ended in the courts. His father did not consider it a proper union in the first place since no priest had been in attendance. He also believed himself to be the injured party in the affair, as the humiliation of his son was from first to last a reflection on him.

To the outward eye, Louis had left no mark upon Cammie; but he did in fact leave at least one: a tattoo high on her right thigh, "Cammie & Louis," inside two hearts that were pierced by an arrow. No one had ever mentioned the marking, but Dr. Camus found it when he was performing the autopsy, after she and her lover had been shot to death outside the Church of the Sacred Heart at the moment the host was consecrated.

*   *   *

He had arrived in town early the previous spring, her lover man, and from the day he appeared, speeding down the main road in a black Ford, fingered throughout his progress by a steady ray of sunlight, people were talking about him. Initially, his physique was less remarkable than his sheer presence, but in a short time, details emerged, and took hold. His hair was slicked, and it was so black it was almost blue, and his suits were all dark; and he stood out against the pale green, just-blossoming trees and hedges like a figure that had been purposefully cut out of the photograph. And so, even when he was there in the flesh, a few hundred yards in front of you, he gave the impression of a man absconded, or repudiated, for reasons you could only guess at. He was broadish-shouldered, yet compact; he had a waist almost ludicrously tapered for a man who was not a professional dancer, and while not very tall, he had a head that was wide and large.

"He has the proportions of a movie star," Thésée Camus pronounced at the time. Thésée was washing his father's car, and he stopped, put his heels together, and gravely made a wide arc with the lathered-up sponge as he spoke. We knew the stranger's name was Lloyd Cannon, from one early encounter: he brought three silk shirts to the laundry to be washed and pressed, and he presented his name, said Noree Rameau, like he'd had it gift-wrapped.

My mother had noticed him herself when she'd gone out with Jeanne-Patrice to look for two yards of navy blue binding tape, and she saw him lounging by his car at the curb. "He was doing nothing, and seemed so unembarrassed about it," she said, disapproving but evidently intrigued. Jeanne-Patrice had had a fresh misfortune with the curling iron that morning, and refused to look up at anybody, and so had no comment to make on the remarkable stranger. But my mother now had a focus worthy of her curiosity, and she applied herself to it with the direction and purpose with which she scrubbed the kitchen floor, or outlined the most recent failings of the local school committee. When the Guild of St Francis met in our kitchen the following Saturday to mend items for a clothing drive, she broached the subject of Lloyd Cannon, his origins and likely goings-on, and waited for the members to reply. I played on the floor with a discarded dishtowel, considered their shoes, and listened.

He was from Oklahoma, they were sure, or Texas, or maybe Arkansas, though old Mrs. Gaultez, who was fond of sunflower seeds, paused with one balanced in the center of her pushed-out lower lip and declared that he had came over the border from Mexico, and was an ex-revolutionary. "He carries the smell of gunpowder upon himself as proudly as an ensign into battle," she said. Then the lip retracted, and the seed disappeared. She picked up her needle again, and recommenced mending a shirt sleeve. Mrs. Carmina thought he had the residual airs and graces of defrocked priest, but Mrs. Leclos said he was too young for that calamity, for, as she pointed out, such a corruption takes time. A number of them voiced their suspicion that he was up to no good, though "no good" was less a definitive judgment than a broad evocation of possibilities.

Mrs. Favereau said she had seen him the day before, wading in the backwater. He was wearing his customary dark suit, and had the pant legs rolled up. When he felt her eyes upon him, she said, he turned and smiled, and he walked out of the water. That was when she saw his right foot was missing the two smallest toes. "He wasn't born like that either," she said, with heavy though indeterminate import. "That flesh bore the cut of metal."

"Like Cinderella's sisters," my mother said, and Mrs. Dubru reached for the scissors and said this man is a heap prettier, with those blue-violet eyes the color of a morning glory. Those eyes belong on a woman, she declared. And most of the time, that's were they're set, Mrs. Carmina said, and they all laughed in a circle, a round or so longer than sounded strictly spontaneous. When she thought they'd had enough, my mother cut in, and asked if anyone would care for an apricot tea square.

In the town's estimation, there was no doubt Lloyd Cannon was a bit of a dandy. He carried upon his person layers of scent: peppermint chewing gum, tobacco, sweat, whiskey, and cologne. He announced himself further through the colors of his shirts, colors that might have been tolerated on a woman: burnt tangerine, robin's egg blue, willow green. But on a man, and in silk, they were deemed everything from reprehensible to ridiculous. They were redolent of the movies, these shirts, and almost oriental in their luxury.

"He looked like a pimp," Gabrielle told me years later, recalling her first sight of him. She had been in her aunt's shop arranging a selection of Boston ferns when she saw him approach the plate glass window, intent on himself and oblivious to all else. A bare inch from the glass, so close he was almost clouding it with his own breath, he stared into his reflection, straightened his hair, and smiled at his own good looks, before he moved on with a faint swagger like one reinvigorated. "I wouldn't have been surprised if he'd asked himself for the next dance," Gabrielle added, with a snort.

Balthezar Broudreau, the police officer, crossed Lloyd's

path on the street soon after his arrival, and passed over him an eye of amused wariness. Some said Balthezar was merely jealous because he had at last met a peacock with brighter plumage on his home turf, but my mother said that was not true. Decorum and understatement had always been the key to Balthezar's code of dressing, she maintained, and when he saw Lloyd Cannon take to the sidewalks of Saint-Baptiste in his gangster's get-up, she was sure Balthezar extended to him the amused indulgence the aristocrat reserves for the parvenu.

In those few weeks he walked the streets of our town, Lloyd Cannon was tagged, variously, as a drifter, a trickster, a gambler, a conman, and a half-wit. Some believed he was fabulously wealthy, because he had no apparent need of work. Others insisted he paid the price of that indolence, and was sleeping in the back of his black Ford car, which he moved to a different spot each night. Everyone wondered what had brought him to this small town. Gabrielle actually asked him, one April twilight outside the superette. Perpetuée and I were at the side of the shop by a patch of bluebells, playing jump rope in the last light of day. A sudden soft wind came up, whispering of rain, and brushed back the glade of flowers like a gloved hand.

"Why, what brought me here, miss, was the peace and quiet and sweet country ways," he said. Then he gave a smile so wide and sudden it made his eyes squint, and it was if the upper part of his face belonged to someone taking aim on a target. He had a way of saying a thing so that you immediately inferred its opposite. My mother, for one, suspected him of a fine piece of irony, countering Gabrielle's nosiness with an answer pointed and smooth. But most people in town seemed to take his response at face-value, and they raised their chin a little at his words, and felt as if they too were seeing Saint-Baptiste for the first time, and breathing in its down-home goodness.

That spring, he was sighted here and there, and initial

opinions of him varied. On the whole, men at first supposed he was stuck on himself, and they were more wary in their estimation, except for Thésée who admired the automobile from afar, and recounted, entranced, its particulars over his family's dinner table. But by all reports from those who had an encounter with him, Lloyd was spirited, community-minded, and solicitous, particularly, everyone felt, for one so questionably attired. The contrast worked to his favor. He waited outside the church when Cammie was at Mass with her mother. Men, especially, respected his masculine forbearance in the matter of church attendance, and a few of them must have envied it. The women, in contrast, regretted his absence, and at Mass I could tell when they were striving to avert their minds from it: they fiddled with the ends of their lace veils, and sang the rejoinder of the Ave Maria more loudly than usual.

A few people reported that when they'd been tramping alone up the long, high, road that led and in out of town, Lloyd drove by, slowed his car, and asked if they needed a lift. He was happy to talk, about the weather, mostly, or baseball, or the superiority of a Ford vehicle over any other make. According to Marc Duane, Lloyd expressed definite opinions to effect that meat loaf is always better on the second day, in a sandwich with unbuttered bread, the crusts still on, and strawberry pie is the waste of a fine summer fruit, a bounty the very reason for which the Lord had seen fit to give us shortcake and whipped cream. But Lloyd was as happy to listen as he was to talk. His passengers found themselves enraptured by his presence, even if they had left his car hours before. The rest of the day, they would impart information, and offer up opinions on a host of subjects, as if Lloyd were still listening at their elbow, and they felt themselves to be knowledgeable, affable, and fascinating.

"He made a person feel wanted," Lazar Monterose told a reporter from the Dallas Times the day after the outlaws were gunned down, "and whatever else he did, he did that too." Lazar then turned back to sweeping up the front porch of his furniture store, the one where the bodies of the slaughtered outlaws had been laid out, late in the afternoon of their ambush and slaughter. After that afternoon, Lazar took to sweeping those floorboards more conscientiously and with a greater sense of purpose than he had ever done before. "They was laid out over there," he said, indicating a corner with his broom head. He told this to those who asked, and to some of those who did not; but beyond that, he would divulge no other corporal detail. If you pressed on, perhaps hoping to cadge some gruesome particular, Lazar slowly drew back his face, hardened his eyes, and tightened his lips, as if some deep suspicion he had always held in your regard had just been confirmed, and he swept on, with a shake of his head.

There was no doubt that children and grown people both felt Lloyd's allure, and even those who condemned him had to admit his charm was at least intermittent, and therefore, all the more dangerous. One afternoon, a few boys gathered for a game of catch on a disused field that adjoined the back of the police building. Lloyd happened by on foot, and without saying a word, slipped off his suit coat, hung it carefully on a fencepost, and took up a baseball mitt. Balthezar Broudreau was passing by, on his way back from his patrol, and he stopped in the shadowy embrace of a flowering pear tree to watch. Lloyd's shirt was buttercup yellow, he said, and shimmered so bright in the sunlight that it was hard to look at him directly for long. The boys at first glanced at each other without nodding assent, and Balthezar wondered if they would simply disperse at Lloyd Cannon's approach. But they carried on with their game, and allowed him to join in.

To the older Charpantier boy, who was nervous and sickly, and when confronted with strangers, pawed the ground like a wayward pony, Lloyd called out encouragement. And, Balthezar reported, the boy looked people in the eye, nearly the whole time, when he visited his daddy's office later that afternoon. René Martin, however, was cocky and inclined to bully his playmates. Lloyd pitched him a ball that curved at the last instant like a hangnail, paused in the air, then dropped heavily at his feet. "René. you could have caught that one," Lloyd called out, and René hung his head in shame, because he knew that it was true. "In that moment, I felt as if this dark stranger had come to the town to expose my weaknesses," René Martin told me, years later, "and I was uneasy in my heart, until I beat up two boys on the way home, and concluded he was nothing but a drifter."

And the butcher Christo Badarde, who had tattoos all over his short fat arms, and faced the world with the soft belly, and the frank, vulnerable eyes, of a child, told how he was stranded just outside the town limits when a tire on his van blew out late one afternoon. Lloyd was driving by. He pulled his car right over onto the timothy grass, got out, and fixed the wheel for him. He showed Christo how to mend the tire, melting the rubber inner tube with the touch of a burnt-out match. Then he stood up, and leaned his back against the side of his Ford, and looked out over the world turning pink in the sunset. The tall grass listed in the wind, Christo said, and Lloyd offered him a stick of chewing gum. Lloyd took one for himself, and told Christo about life.

Christo mentioned the encounter to a couple of people the story the day it happened, and no one questioned his account. But later, after the outlaws had been gunned down, and their significance to us was as undoubted as it was undefined, he took to adding details that he had not related before. Christo said that as Lloyd fixed the tire, he cocked his head to one side, and talked about his own daddy, how he'd worked now and then on a road crew, and Lloyd had loved the smell of hot tar ever since, hankered after it, because it reminded him of when his daddy was in work, and there would be fried chicken and peach pie for supper. But later on, Christo also came to recall Lloyd's comments on the nature of man versus the rest of creation ("'animals don't hate, and we're supposed to better than them'"), and the inestimable virtues of Maxwell House coffee: (""I'll tell you something, it *is* good to the last drop.'") Over the years, as Christo's recollection of the encounter multiplied in detail, and several of the advertising slogans he referenced were from impossibly recent campaigns, people came to doubt him, and no longer wished to hear his stories. When they passed him on the road, they took to hurrying by, and Christo's eyes grew sad, bewildered, and old.

In those few weeks of the stranger's appearance, no one had anything very bad to report of him. It was noted he had taken a particular shine to Cammie. Over all, that counted in his favor, and the town watched, and wondered what would become of them.

I saw them together one Saturday just before Easter. I like to imagine it was the very first time they met, and I have reason to believe that it was. I had woken up earlier than anyone else, as was my custom in those years, dressed quickly, and went downstairs to the back hall. I was after the fishing rod my brother Henri had been piecing together the night before last. I found it, stashed below the canned tomatoes, under a couple of musty raincoats. I nabbed my mother's old straw hat, the one she wore when she was out weeding the back garden, from its hook on the pantry door; and, while my family was above me sleeping, I slipped out.

But I had no luck, standing there ankle-deep in brackish weeds, under the warmth of a yellowish sun, and the oversized brim of the purloined hat. After what I suppose was about an hour of it, I decided to go to LaFarge's superette by the backroad and get myself a cold root beer. The road was lined on either side with pine, and the air was thin and sweet, and smelled of spring. A half mile or so down, on my left, there was an abandoned fish cannery, a large terracotta-colored building that no longer had any roof, door or windows; and as I was passing by, Iphigénie Camus emerged from the bluish-green overgrowth that surrounded it inside and out.

She came towards me, half friendly, half ashamed, like a dog who isn't sure if it will be petted or whipped, so wags its tail and hangs its head in equal measure. She was done up for Easter already, it appeared, with a pink dress and a dangling hair ribbon to match, which she pulled at from time to time. I said hello without commitment, and kept walking, and Iphigénie trailed behind me, asking over and over in her whiny breathless repetitive way that seemed to trail to the ground and get caught under your feet, how many fish did I catch that day, that sure is a fine hat, could she try it on huh please. I ignored her because I knew that was what she hated most. I turned the corner, and a small breeze kicked up, cool as air released from an uncorked bottle of pop, and the grass stirred like something breathing.

He was standing there, in a grove of crimson crepe myrtle. "Lloyd Cannon," he was saying, a rising clamour to his voice, as if the very fact of so being was a hoot he had just elected to share with the rest of the world. He had his arms stretched out for emphasis. Iphigénie shut up, and sidled in closer, and I noticed that, in repose her tragic brow seemed more heavy than ever. Lloyd was leaned up against the side of his black Ford, and he and the car imposed themselves with the very blackness of their forms against the burgeoning green. He took no notice of us, because he was talking to Cammie, who stood a few feet away. Her dress was Nile green, the breeze was playing at its hem, and she'd put her head to one side to listen to him.

Lloyd was chewing gum, and he deployed it like rapid-fire line of punctuation to his smile and his talk: a dash, a question mark, an exclamation point. He was talking on and on. "Some cheap palaver" was the phrase I remember thinking, but I suspect that was a judgment I picked up afterwards. His talk was smart; by turns fast and slow; and as tantalizing as a half-forgotten song playing on a radio in some distant yard. You stopped to listen to it. The gist was he was he was surely pleased to meet her this fine morning, and even those banal words of his seemed enter onto the spring air smelling of his cologne. And Cammie ducked her head, her laugh rang out, and she was done for. I don't think they ever knew we were standing there, Iphigénie and I, like deer at the edge of a forest. Having seen enough of the ways of man, we retreated the way we had come.

Afterwards, they were seen around town, or more properly, travelling through it. If I squinted and tried to see Saint-Baptiste the way I imagined they did then, the town reconfigured to nothing but a view from a car window, flat as a postcard; and the roads became less a measure of space than of time, and were in any case only the conduit through which their love progressed. We'd catch sight of them in Lloyd's car, whizzing along the main thoroughfare. Or, if you thought you'd finally caught a glimpse of Cammie on her own, choosing a bottle of soda at LaFarge's, you'd look out and realize Lloyd was there, waiting at the curb in the car with the engine running, cleaning his teeth in the rear view mirror, and grinning every so often to check his progress. Or you might venture just beyond the town limits on the north line, where strawberries grew wild and you could pick and eat until your belly went queasy; and suddenly feel the weight of their gaze upon you from some unsuspected corner. All there was for a decent person to do was to get moving. "I guess I ain't decent," Gabrielle said, and maintained she'd continue to stare flatly.

Then the two were gone, as if a cloud of dust had spun up on the road and spirited them away, automobile and all. Mrs. Favereau said Lloyd Cannon was an enchanter in the real sense of the word, because first he had conjured himself up, and then he made the both of them disappear. After that, and in a matter of months, they came back to us in the headlines.

They left behind the entire town, and she'd left, in particular, two folks, her mother and Louis. In later years, I used to imagine how she had haunted them in her absence: Louis would be in the midst of estimating the cost of a roof repair, when a whiff of some perfume, almost too sweet to bear, reached his nostrils. He'd put down his pencil, sigh, and think of Cammie. Or, at the whistle of some train in the distance, the mother would raise her head, and wonder where Cammie was at that very moment, what she was doing, and if she was happy. I was convinced that Cammie in recollection, perhaps even more than in proximity, had the effect of bending one's mind towards the clichés of popular ballads. She was the source from which such ballads sprang.

In truth, her mother appeared little affected by Cammie's absconding. She had already survived her daughter's ill-starred marriage to Louis. Some said Mrs. Roux hovered a bit longer at the door of LaFarge's, and people watched to see if she was lonely, or ashamed, and if that loneliness or shame was driving her to madness and ruin, but there was no real evidence one way or the other.

As for Louis, he went so pale, you felt that if you cut into him, his blood would leak out the color of new-wood sap. If ever her name was mentioned in his presence, people looked at their shoes, or far down the road, and looked back only after a new subject had been brought up and was safely underway. Louis clipped a sprig of baby's breath from her bouquet, and kept it enclosed within a pocket-sized volume of classical quotations.

One night, in that short, spring season of Lloyd Cannon, Gabrielle ran across the book by chance. She had been leafing through it, she told me, bored after making the beds and sweeping the floors, and wondered if anybody had ever thought to say an interesting thing about housework, when the shriveled stems, delicate as a desiccated spider's web, slid halfway out. Years later, I asked her at what page Louis had hidden the sprig, because I hoped its placement would reveal to me some secret of his heart. It was a Roman poet from the time of Julius Caesar, Gabrielle said with disgust, though, no doubt to sustain her disgust, as was her custom and desire, she could still recall the quotation: "Let him who never loved before find love tomorrow; and may he who has already loved, find love tomorrow too." She brought the book down from her shelf, turned to the page, and showed it to me. The editors had appended a parenthetical note, in minuscule italic, that the remarks were attributed to Catullus. For me, the quote's significance was in the annotation: it was that touch of the secondary and the uncertain that struck me as so very like Louis.

"What I can never forgive him is his wilfulness," Gabrielle told me that night. It was strange, for most people said what Louis lacked was a will of his own. She seemed to know what I was thinking. "Don't let the snivellers fool you," she said. She was washing dishes at the sink, and had her face half-turned towards me. "They always get their way in the end, don't they?"

She was in the habit of posing questions that had no need of an answer. In her conversation, they often sufficed as greetings and farewells, and in response, I said nothing, and wondered if, from her point of view, and judging by the angle of her profile, my visit had reached its conclusion. But still I wondered what was it Louis could have willed, that day of the First Communion that the shots rang out, and the little brides and grooms of Christ ran down the church steps, in white and cream and ivory, and darkened their sleeves with the blood of the town's slaughtered outlaws.

III

On the morning he was to leave the town forever, and render us our enduring legend, Louis Sante had awoken early, opened his bedroom window a few inches, and splashed a handful of cold water onto his face. It was a couple of weeks after his seventeenth birthday. Gabrielle remembered he rose that day before the cocks had crowed, and she heard the window screech and stick as he jimmied it upwards. She thought Louis must have had business in the next town. He eked a living together mending fences, painting houses, and repairing roofs. He was a willing worker at all tasks, and his face was as pleasant and shy and unperturbed as the sun coming out after a spring shower as he gazed at whatever object needed repair, and estimated how long the work would take him; but roofs were far and away his favorite.

"The boy did hunger after height," Gabrielle said. "If he'd been born in New York City, he'd have been a steeplejack on the skyscrapers, but as it was, he climbed ladders, and balanced himself on the eaves, and that's where he seemed most at peace: atop a roof, and alone."

As Gabrielle lay in bed that morning, she could already feel the day's heat gathering. It was taking shape like a wild creature, she said, though at that hour it had not yet deigned to stir its limbs. She heard the clump of her brother's boots going down the staircase. The back door creaked open, and slammed shut. A motor revved up. Then she went back to sleep. "I was dreaming I was being fitted for an evening gown," she said. "It was bias-cut, and midnight blue with just a hint of sparkle, like an ice skater's costume. It cooled me off just to picture it. I could feel the swish of the fabric as it moved." She gestured as I spoke to her that afternoon all those years later, and I understood that the dress was to have been set off by gloves that reached over the elbow.

On that day he was to become a traitor, a murderer, and a maker of legends, Louis slipped on a denim shirt that was so washed out it was almost white, and a pair of jeans that were stiff and indigo. Those jeans were what Gabrielle referred to as his "dress denims," and the question eventually arose as to what event did he have in mind that morning which required him to dress with an eye to both practicality and mild formality. He also tucked a Colt .45 into his belt.

When his father woke a few hours later, with much on his mind and a purpose at hand, he rummaged around in the back closet for his gun, and in the process, woke up Gabrielle. The empty hangers rattled icily; but he could not find what he was looking for, and a cold gray sweat broke out on his face like a hard frost out of season. Some speculated, on the basis of the purloined firearm, that Louis intended to join with the forces of law, and fire upon the bandits himself. Others insisted that he had surmised what was in store, and, determined to thwart his father's schemes as best he could, spirited away the most trusted firearm in the house, as he set out for parts unknown. Investigators and reporters would go on to term the Colt .45, which was never found and so existed only in the memories of the father and the records of police, "The Phantom Gun." In later years, Mrs. Favereau, a spiritualist and the mother of the town druggist, would claim to hear its rat-a-tat-tat in the small hours of morning. But since she also said she had encountered the Czar strolling down the main street of the town one New Year's Eve, his beard snow white and a liver-spotted whippet by his side, she was largely dismissed with a shrug of the shoulders.

All agreed, however, that whatever his reason for taking the pistol on that particular day, keeping company with guns was resolutely out of character. Louis had not participated in so much as a turkey hunt since he was twelve years old. His father could recall the day of that failed hunt with bitter shame, how Louis wept on the way out to the dun-colored woods, and, on the way back, trailed, sniffling, behind the men and the dead birds slung over their shoulders. He limped through the frozen grass. By then, his character had taken form, and its inclinations were apparent: Louis was mild-mannered, dispirited, and luckless in all affairs of the heart. He was filial, fraternal, and haplessly romantic.

The spring that the outlaws were shot down was warm and wet. The hay in the barns turned to rot, and through the sheets of falling rain, the smell hung in the air, sweet, and putrid. So long did spring go on, and so slow was summer to arrive, that the drugstore ran out of Dr. Peterson's Famous Mayday Cardiac Tonic for Females, and the unquelled palpitations of the heart seemed to migrate straight down to old ladies's feet, which fidgeted mightily but futilely upon being directed straight into muddy puddles (for, short of staying home, there no way to avoid them that year). Perpetuée had planted a row of white French violets in the front hedge, delving into dark soil so moist it almost gurgled when she cut into it. Within hours, a heavy torrent swept the plants away. She watched open-mouthed and helpless from the window, and her father shrugged, smiled, his face reflected dimly in the greenish pane of glass, and said, perhaps they were homesick, and would take root in some more hospitable *terroir.* He was given to such gnomic comments, and opinion in town was divided as to whether he was wise, or sly, or merely annoying. Perpetuée at this juncture appeared to opt for last. She pointed at the disappearing stream of water and dirt and plant root, and howled.

And that whole spring, while the rain fell and the hay rotted, love was eating away at Louis's heart like a worm in a rose. His face drained to a humid whitish-green, and his deep brown eyes went sorrowful and mild. So saintly was his suffering, and so completely did he take to it, that he could have been the model for any of a number of figures in the stained glass windows of the Church of the Sacred Heart. No one dared mention the progress of the outlaw couple to him, because we all bore in mind, in case he did not, the fact that just a year before, Cammie had stood with him before a justice of the peace, in a dress of dotted swiss with the bodice too low and the hem unravelling in front, and for a few hours before the sun rose and his father found out, became his bride.

"She didn't have a church of her own to go to," Gabrielle Sante said. "And she was dressed in red polka dots. Nothing she did after that could surprise me much."

Gabrielle and Louis lived with their widowed father in a sand-colored ramshackle house with paint peeling off its scalloped shingles, and a front gate that never latched proper, and was bedeviled by every passing wind. Whenever I came near the Sante house, I hurried by, for the place filled me with gloom and foreboding. A fringe of dark shrubs defended the front yard, and the house bordered a disused road that even then was no wider than a footpath. The vines overhead had sprung up so thick and twisted and shadowy that the path was cast into permanent twilight. The landscape around the Santes was not so much wild and untouched as overgrown and gone to seed. It was as if, at the wrong touch of finger, or of breath, some fruit on point of rotting would fall to the ground, set seed, and yield yet more putrefaction.

On warm spring nights, the sky lavender and wet-looking, the father sat out on the porch. He took in the smell of the bougainvillea, and dreamt of the stock market. He was in the habit of saving the business section of the newspaper for last, Gabrielle told me, and only after scanning the news from the state capital, and the fortunes of the local baseball team did he take the business page, with its array of tiny figures in columns, and draw it within an inch of his nose. According to his daughter, the very phrase "stock market" appealed to him; and I could believe it, its abstractness almost lyrical, and its magic wrapped up in seeming everydayness and so all the more potent: "the market" - where you bought not a pork chop, a dozen apples, or a quart of milk, but commodities, and a piece of the future.

Its crash some five years back had only increased its romantic allure to him; for now it was like a house not only with many mansions, but also half-ruined. His daydreams, I am sure, abounded with silos spilling over with golden grain, stockades of cattle, white-breathed and hot-blooded in the cold black void of a Chicago dawn, and endless bolts of textiles lined up in some dusty warehouse. Sometimes, an owl would hoot from the dark line of trees in the distance, or Gabrielle would open the screen door and ask if he wanted a tip of brandy; and Mr Sante raised his head from the newspaper, gave momentary heed, and went on speculating.

He ghost-invested in stocks, and wrote out each of his investments on a scrap of paper. After a period of deliberation, for which he required absolute silence, he put down an amount, then he affixed his signature and the date. Though he tormented himself with what he would have gained in investments if they had been real he did not console himself with what he would have lost in all the others.

He was a clerk in the town tax office, and had been installed there by his wife's family in the wake of his engagement to her. In all his years there, he advanced more slowly than most, but in time he was to catch up. Within a few months of the death of the outlaws, Sante skipped four grades in a single promotion. This was a move which raised eyebrows among the knowing, who knew best of all how to keep silent. He was given a desk as broad and empty as a Great Plains state, and an office with a bay window that in spring let in the smell of cape jasmine. By Christmas, he moved house, to an antique-pink colonial with a white veranda that curved around the front like a scroll of meringue. Gabrielle refused to go with him.

She packed up and went to live with her aunt, and tended the flower shop alongside her. "I would rather arrange flowers than deaths," Gabrielle told her father. In later years, when she told the story, she took to adding: "and ferny greens than betrayals." She had been reading a number of true confession magazines, and the phrase had just come to her as she stood on the sagging front porch of his old house for the last time. Her wording pleased her, and inspired to live up to its elegance, she readjusted her hat. As she walked down the front steps, her head held high, a tin can lying in the gutter was taken up by a stray wind, and it rattled down the empty road.

In those years before the death of the outlaws, Sante made his home with his son and daughter. He kept a photo of his wife on his bedside table, beside the water tumbler that held his teeth at night. Her face was a small, gardenia-shaped blur of white, and it was fading year by year into the sepia sunlight of some winter's afternoon he could no longer rightly place. She had died giving birth to Gabrielle.

Whenever his mother's name was mentioned, Louis's eyes watered mightily, and he looked as though something was stepping on the toes of his heart, but he was too steadfast to draw attention to the infraction and withstood its agony like a stalwart tin soldier come halfway to life but no further.

Gabrielle, on the other hand, stuck out her chin out like a front stoop. She told you that, as a matter of fact, her mother had never seen her only daughter draw her first breath, she had died so quick. Then she asked you a string of questions on the order of: is the fifth wedding anniversary the one for clocks or paper, or is that third; are Gravensteins or Baldwins or Rome Beauties the best apples to use in a pie; of Prussian blue, della robbia, and periwinkle, which is the most seemly for a girl's first formal gown? Before there was any answer, Gabrielle would frown, and we gathered that those were the kind of questions her momma could have answered had she lived, but since she hadn't, her daughter was cast adrift in the world asking uninformed and befuddled folks the number of cups per pound in a measure of brown sugar, and of white. All the while Gabrielle was posing those questions, her voice took on a progressive sigh, until it weren't nothing but; meanwhile, her eyes, the color of cool green grapes, faced you down like a brick wall, or a dare.

Gabrielle's maternal aunt, Sophia, who ran the local flower shop, maintained stoutly that not having children was the only way to ensure that a woman led a long life. Of course, Cammie Roux, childless and gunned down before she was twenty, was the exception that proved the rule.

"No womb, full or empty, untried or distended from constant use, could shield anyone from that hail of gunfire," Sophia said. She had a misfortune with the eyebrow pencil that day. The line that had been sharp and true in the morning had melted with the day's humidity and blood-spattered tumult, and this failure gave a distracted, desperate air to a face that was already, by long-established habit, overly-knowing. She took a sip of tea, and wrinkled her small nose in satisfaction.

At this talk of wombs, Sante cleared his throat, took a sudden interest in swatting a fly that wasn't there, and generally made enough noise to drown out what he was pretending he hadn't heard in the first place. But afterward, people began to wonder if it was not the mention of female organs at all, but his role in the hail of gunfire that had taken place on the road outside the church that afternoon that made him so ill at ease. At that point, no one knew that Louis was lost to the town forever, but everyone knew he had certainly given it much to talk about.

For, early on the morning before the killings, by the side of a tar-topped road that stretched like a run-over black snake along the swollen backwater, Louis had made his peace with a local police officer, Balthezar Broudreau. Gabrielle had spotted them when she'd been on her way to her aunt's flower shop. They were leaning against the police car by the side of the road, and looking off into the hazy mid-distance.

"I was annoyed," she said, "because Louis was supposed to be at Rachette's farm that very minute, plugging up a drained well, but instead he just stood there with an armed officer of the law, doing nothing. Also, the backwater stunk of rotting fishgut by that hour, and it gave me a headache just to be near it."

She watched as the officer offered Louis a cigarette. They smoked in silence, and it did seem to her that an agreement of some form had taken place. The smoke floated upon the air, she said, undisturbed, as though setting a seal upon an understanding.

By sundown of the day on which the outlaws had been blasted to bits outside the church, she had convinced herself that there had been an arrangement, and that the arrangement had been this: Louis was to lure the outlaw couple to some agreed-upon field or forest or turn in a road, where the assembled forces of justice would fire upon the man, but not the girl. Nor, when the time came was Gabrielle the only member of the town to suspect that the outlaws had been set up that day. Some were attracted

43

to the thought, some repulsed, and most, truth to be told, intoxicated with a mixture of both. Afterwards, when they thought more clearly about the matter, many wondered aloud how even Louis could have been so witless as to suppose gunfire could be controlled in such circumstances, and, that even if the lawmen could aim so straight, they'd have the will to do as they'd promised.

For a very brief while, Louis's role as lover and betrayer was the main focus of speculation, and the death of the outlaws entered as but a refrain in the ballad of Louis Sante. Many drew attention to the rumor that Louis had been sighted around town that morning armed with a gun, and they drew various conclusions from that. According to Octave Dubru, Louis knew the police were assembling, and on his own, had resolved to protect the couple; or, in an alternate version, to protect just the girl. Others believed Louis was looking to shoot Lloyd for what he gotten Cammie into; and a hardy few, that Louis intended to shoot himself in view of the girl, to show her what she had done to him. This most vocal proponent of this last account was old Mrs. Gaultez, who scanned the radio dial after midnight for a station deep inside the Mexican border that broadcast sad and endless songs of love and tragedy.

My brother Henri put forth the notion that Louis wanted to shoot Cammie Roux himself so no one else would ever have her. He said this one night over the dinner table, trying it out, and looked around at us for our reaction to his outburst of mature and new-found insight. My father looked back at him over the platter of leftover pork chops going cold, his jaws working away on his supper with melancholy steadiness, and he said nothing. Henri dropped his gaze, and mumbled it was just something that he'd heard. Personally, I believe that Louis had a gun, but no intention of firing it. In my view, the gun was not a badge of defiance, but of defeat; and I imagine it glinting in the morning light like a flag of surrender, pocket-sized, for convenience, and made of metal, for durability.

And as time went on, Louis came to be seen as more an agent of haplessness than of treachery. The weight of opinion was that, in the end, the outcome was down to Cammie. As many pointed out, even if Louis had come to some kind of agreement with the police, it was no doubt Cammie who had made Lloyd drive by the Church of the Sacred Heart. Some believed that she knew what was in wait, and wanted to die by Lloyd's side, and if Louis was there to witness it, so much the better.

In later years, one of the armed officers brought in from Texas wrote that, just before the shots rang out, Cammie turned to look at Louis, who was standing in the shadows of a willow tree. Her neck was straight, and her eyes dead-level and fearless, like a barbarian queen delivered to the scaffold. And Louis knew, the lawman wrote, that in that gaze was Lloyd's triumph, and her own.

But as Théramène pointed out, this lawman had misspelled the name of several surrounding towns, and attributed cornflower blue eyes to Charpantier, when they were clearly green. Mrs. Roux never raised a herd of spotted pigs, and Cammie had never kept a dog called Asterix. The lawman referred to the event as not merely a tragedy but as "Shakespearean" - largely, Théramène guessed, for no better reason than he hankered after a polysyllabic adjective. Moreover, and this was Théramène's *coup de grâce*, delivered with a dismissive shrug of his shoulders, and a faint smile, which invited his listener to join him in a moment of gratified disdain, the work was self-published. And that, so far as Théramène was concerned, consigned the images of a jilted lover waiting for death in a grove of trees, and a condemned barbarian queen, back to the novelettes and song lyrics and true confessions from which they had no doubt emerged.

I believe Gabrielle was wrong in concluding that Louis had conspired against the outlaw couple. It was typical of her to cast the doings of others in the light of her own untrusting disposition. Balthezar and Louis were simply having a cigarette when she caught sight of them by the water. It was not Louis but his father who cut the deals in that family; and Balthezar himself had already come to the conclusion that whatever determinations Louis ever made would be indelibly overwritten by his father's. However, in the event, Sante ruled, but he also failed. Charged with the responsibility of keeping an eye on Louis that day, he slept late while his son got up and went abroad into the land. The eyes of too many fathers were shut that day, Théramène remarked to me thirty-four years later, and cast about his desktop for a pencil to jot the phrase down.

Over time, no one apart from Gabrielle believed that Louis promised anything to Balthezar other than to intervene with the outlaws, if he should see them, and beseech them to surrender. It was simply not in character for Balthezar to seek armed confrontation. At an outdoor rifle festival the previous fall, Balthezar had gone on record saying that he found gunfire discordant.

But by the time one hundred-sixty-seven rounds of shot riddled the outlaws and their car just outside the First Communion at the Church of the Sacred Heart, singeing the sweet mock-orange, and scattering the road with scores of lead pellet, it had became evident that Balthezar was better suited to face the aftermath of the incident than Charpantier. Balthezar did not sweat under its glare, but glowed. He appeared to welcome it as graciously as he would the return of an errant friend.

*   *   *

Balthezar Broudreau had soft, sorry eyes the color of a caramel left out all week to the sun and rain, and a swooping moustache nearly the same shade that reached to his collar. He was slight physically, but exact sartorially, neat not so much as a pin as a knife blade, and near as sharp. His uniform was always freshly pressed, his shoes polished to a high shine, and his hat angled just so. If you watched him closely as he patrolled the town center, nine to one you'd catch him slow his pace as he passed by the plate windows of the five and dime on the main street, and caught an eyeful of himself, suited up the color of an iced tea, his gun riding comfortably on his hip and glinting in the yellow sunlight. Unlike the most men's vanity, the sight of himself did not blind him to the world; rather, it inspired him, filled him with a slow and measured confidence, and gave him insight into the minds of others. As he would subsequently declare to the *Saint-Baptiste Gazette*: "I acted not simply as an officer of the law, but as an eyewitness to the human condition." A reporter then moved in to take his photo, the brownie held high above the crowd like a holy object for all to see, but Balthezar raised a hand, and said he needed a moment first, "out of regard for your readers." Then he took a tortoise-shell comb and a miniature mirror out of his pocket, and attended to his needs, and evidently, our own. When the picture was snapped, the camera gave off a cloud of smoke, and it rankled in the air and upon our tongues like an aftertaste of the burned cordite from the gunfire a few hours earlier.

Eleven years in the police force had deepened the lines around Balthezar's mouth, and his sense of his own gravitas. His eyes held an accumulating pity for the affairs of men. At one point, he might have gone into the priesthood, my mother said (they had been in the same class at school); but only if he could have started at the Vatican, and been named straightaway a papal nuncio. One day when they were in the sixth grade, my mother came across him in the back aisle of the gloomy, high-ceilinged public library. Opened on the table in front of him was *L'Encylopedie catholique*, and he was sat, musing over pagefuls of four-color engraved illustrations of officers of the church. The table of vestments held an especial attraction for him. He pointed to each item, and into the humid half-light, whispered its precise and proper name: brevet, cassock, miter. The panoply of outfitting seemed to give Balthezar heart; made him feel that there was a glorious order to the world, and that dressing up to it was a gesture of respect and love directed not so much towards oneself as towards that ordered world. His dandyism, in short, was not that of an egoist, but of an altruist, of a believer in human society, and, further, one who aspired to so believe.

It was in the darkness of the Saint-Baptiste Majestic theater that Balthezar found his purpose in life revealed to him. The lower stall of the movie house was shrouded in shadows, stuffed with velvet upholstery, and adorned with rosewood carvings.

"It's like a confessional," he told my mother.

In that sanctioned dark, he said, he both laughed and cried, and was both alone, and in the company of others. As my mother recalled it, Balthezar had begun failing Latin after the fourth year. "He was disastrous with the ablative," she said, "and had no conception of the pluperfect tense." Classical grammar stood as something of an ideal for Balthezar, but it never became a practice; and in those final years of school, he no doubt began rethinking his future as the reels of film unfolded in the hushed and velvet dark around him.

One day he saw a movie starring a young actor named McAllister Reid. Reid played a special services policeman who is eventually compelled to turn in his own long-lost younger brother. Throughout the course of withstanding impertinences from criminals, and looking after his elderly émigré of a father (near death, but newly invigorated upon the return of his wayward second son), Reid was not only morally righteous, but as elegant as any gangster he faced down. He wore a suit that was casual and sharp, and appropriate to all seasons. Balthezar committed the cut of the shoulder to memory, and wondered about the heft of the wool. In the climatic scene, which came after the policeman had left his father's deathbed, and was snapping handcuffs onto his felonious brother, Reid looked to the heavens, and the words on the title card followed: "Father forgive me." Then the actor's face filled the screen big as a canned ham, Balthezar said, but the sentiment gave it wings.

Thereafter, moral dilemmas posing duty to state against loyalty to family became a favorite of Balthezar's. He speculated over them, and under their influence, sighed with a world-weary indulgence for all things mortal. Everyone in town knew, however, that Balthezar would never turn in a member of his own extensive and sleepy-eyed clan, no matter what. Like Latin grammar, rule of law was an ideal he respected, but did not strictly enforce. It was honorable and sophisticated for a public official to have such sentiments, he seemed to say with his half-smile, and wave of his hand; and in time, he proceeded through the streets of Saint-Baptiste, trailing his shadow alongside himself, as rich in ambiguity and moral complexity as any Vatican appointee. His last year in school, he had begun walking about with his shoulders thrown back like a young cadet, or a man being fitted by a tailor; and upon graduation, he joined the local police force. His widowed mother, who had long envisioned her only son as a monseigneur at the very least, bore the disappointment like a mortal, lingering wound to the chest, and took to sitting all day on her shadowy front porch, chewing on oranges, spitting out the seeds, and refusing to wave at passing cars.

The bandit couple drew together all his knowledge of the human heart. Balthezar ran their story through his mind like a half-forgotten lyric, which he conspired to have return to him and settle upon him in its totality, largely through the act of not moving. While his colleagues tracked the outlaws's movements on a large wall map with red, yellow and green pins, for shoot-outs, robberies, and mere sightings thereof; while they arranged meetings and they waved their arms about and stood up and held forth on the significance of the sighting of a pearl gray Ford in Alibelene the week before, and their rivals raised a skeptical eyebrow, and championed an alternative sighting over in Little Rock; while they did all this and more, Balthezar sipped coffee at his desk, savored a cream horn or two, and smiled.

His clerical studies had hardly gone to waste, for had they not taught him that the stone that the builders rejected became the cornerstone? (Passed over for promotion twice already, Balthezar took comfort in the words. "What irony," he told a reporter later, "that the maxim proved a lodestar for my own conjecture regarding the celebrated outlaws.") Balthezar turned his thoughts away from the bandits directly, their bloody career, known hangouts, and likely targets, and towards, instead, the lost and grieving bridegroom left behind; and finally, one further step aside, that boy's father.

It took no genius to say that Sante loved his son, for what father did not; but what Balthezar divined further was the specific pitch and tone of the love Sante bore him. He had seen them around town, the son hesitant, and appearing to stand off to one side of his very self, the father so impatient with him that his face took on a fierce smile that seized up his features like ice overtaking the gears of a combine.

Balthezar had witnessed such an exchange in what he referred to as "the Incident in the Saint-Baptiste Post Office." (Louis had failed to attach adequate postage to a box of pecan turtles addressed to a great auntie celebrating her 81st birthday in the next parish, and the box languished two days in the post office of origin). Standing behind his son, Sante caught eyes with the postal clerk, and, in Balthezar's words, attempted to "forge a conspiracy of indulgent disdain between them." The incident brought the father and son into focus for Balthezar.

He reckoned, finally, that Sante loved Louis the way

you love an imbecile offspring, or your own body's degenerating and imperfect flesh: dismay mingled with tenderness, apprehension with pity, and shame and annoyance with stark cold terror. In Balthezar's opinion, Sante was like a man who glimpses his corporal decay in a mirror and feels the cold and sudden stab of mortality, and he was perpetually searching for an ally over and above the encroaching inadequacy that looked back at him. With a dispassionate eye, Balthezar had concluded thus: in relation to a son, a father has already created, he was bound to protect, but, for as long as he could, he reserved the right to destroy. Balthezar knew that if any project regarding Louis was to come to pass, it had to be backed in full by the father.

And, as emerged in the course of his discussion with Sante, Balthezar had once been to New Orleans, and seen the trading at the cotton market. He scarcely noticed the pilot light of interest that was sparked in Sante's eyes, but nonetheless that interest kept at a steady burn. Fénelon Favereau the druggist overheard them, and after the outlaws were shot outside the Church of the Sacred Heart, and the woman's front tooth blown to splinters by a direct hit, he talked about it to anyone who would listen, reluctant to blurt out what he knew, but more than willing to be coaxed into disclosing it.

They'd been holed up in the café, Balthezar and Sante, long enough to be on their second cup of coffee. They were sitting next to each other by the bar, directly under the revolving ceiling fan. The heat was already beginning, and the humidity building up, like a wall of stone. The rain was still falling that day, a Tuesday, Favereau remembered, but lightly, and it rattled intermittently on the tin roof. Roland the fisherman sat at his accustomed place in the corner. Singing rose from the direction of the church. Balthezar said it sounded like a wedding was underway. Sante snorted in response. Then Favereau, who had only dropped in to pick up a sandwich, heard Balthezar begin to speak.

"He was like a priest with a litany," Favereau said. "Some words came out soft and other ones louder, some were rushed and some slowed down, but whichever they were, they kept on coming." Balthezar let unfurl a ribbon of speech about a church service he'd heard once in New Orleans, and how, in comparison, the cotton market was positively sedate. Sante looked up at him an instant. But Balthezar did not see the look, Favereau said, because by then he had tilted his head toward the window again. He listened a moment, shook his head, and said that marriage mingles the blood of two families, for good or ill.

As the fan overhead turned slowly, and without cease, a thought must have taken shape in Sante's head. I pictured it coming in the form of a sentence, and circling his mind like a toy airplane buzzing around a toy globe: "They aren't like us, that pair, not like my family and not like this entire town."

"I ain't got a thing to do with them," he said; it has never been certain whether the "them" referred to the outlaws, or to Cammie and Louis, or to the couple whose wedding chorus he might have been overhearing. In any case, Sante watched the fan as it completed one revolution and began the next. He raised his right hand into the air, like a man taking an oath, and told Balthezar, "My blood will be unspoilt, whatever the cost." Or he may have said "un-spilt," because, when questioned about it afterwards, Favereau, who had always been a nervous mouse of a man, with tiny, fretful hands, frowned, and tugged at his watch chain.

Whatever the case, Balthezar coughed, and with a nod to the silent café keeper, ordered another couple of black coffees. At this point, Favereau hurried outside; though he had ordered a chicken sandwich, and been given ham, he thought the better of it. He was discomfited at the talk of blood (it was the sole reason he had became a druggist and not a doctor, his mother had always said, to anyone who would listen), and fled into the light of day. The bells on the door rattled loudly after him, he said, and he noticed that Charpantier, the local sheriff, was standing by himself in front of the barbershop across the square. When Balthezar entered Favereau's drugstore a half hour later, slowly proceeding down the soap aisle, and pausing to purchase a bottle of aspirin, he was as calm and self-possessed as ever. To Favereau the overhearer, condemned in the town's memory to be forever nibbling on the conversations of others, this much was apparent: Balthezar believed that, having secured the crucial resolve of the father, an end to the matter was in sight. And as he sauntered with a half-smile among the falling-down stacks of crackerjack, Balthezar seemed to imagine that end would be peaceable.

Balthezar had not seen, and did not suspect "the thousand machinations of Charpantier," as he would later term them. But Favereau was not the only one to remark upon Charpantier's presence on the main street that morning; and Favereau's account, though seemingly as bland and open and featureless as the sheriff's own face, reminded others of where they had seen Charpantier throughout that day, who he was with, and what counsel he took.

Charpantier had been sheriff for about two years. He had a frank, corpulent face, with a cast of pink across it like the beginning of a sunburn, and a glint of silver-blond stubble that surfaced by four o'clock and caught the afternoon light. His eyes were yellow-green, and the effect of their startling color was only heightened by their expression, which was unfailingly candid, curious, and merry. He had wide haunches that were too solidly fat to wobble much, and short legs that tapered to small, neat feet. Altogether, he looked like a pig from the pages of a children's story book, who goes about on two legs, wears breeches, and speaks succinctly and with hard common sense. This was an impression I could never shake. When

Charpantier stood on the speaker's platform at the Saint-Bapitiste nameday fair, his badge pinned lopsidedly over his heart, and announced the winner of the day's raffle, he would slap his belly for emphasis, and I could not help but imagine the succulent hiss Charpantier's fat would make on a barbeque spit. I think he would have understood, too, if I had ever told him. He had no illusions, he liked to say, as if he were dispelling ours by the act of saying it.

Charpantier regarded the world as if it were a comedian desperate to amuse him, but only moderately successful at the task. His first day in town (for he hailed from a district forty miles to the northwest, famed for its dust, its lack of alcohol, and its herds of Friesian cattle), he was met at the train station by a delegation of notables led by Balthezar. Balthezar wore a pair of suede gloves the color and texture of fresh-churned butter, and a light straw hat with a brim as wide as a manhole cover. He greeted the new sheriff with a politeness so courtly that it could not help but flatter the giver rather than the receiver. Charpantier looked at him, and turned as square as he was, his belly seemed to be looking too. (A photo of this moment appeared in the town paper, like a tableau of mismatched chess pieces, with a short caption; my father had driven the reporter up to Port-Royale once, and he knew the whole story.) Charpantier was too bored to respond to Balthezar, and too amused to look away, and the space of silence grew uncomfortably wide. Father Ducie then stepped forward, the hem of his cassock tremulous in the slight breeze, and intimated that this Officer Balthezar Broudreau was a man of learning, and near clerical cultivation.

"Thank you kindly," Charpantier said, not moving his eyes from Balthezar's face, "Otherwise I might have thought he was a pansy." Charpantier took a congenial chew on his tobacco, and spit a long brown stream into a blush-pink azalea planted along the platform. Then he smiled, and his smile hit them in the face like the broadside slap of a sword. To the end of his days, he was cheerful, patient, and brutal.

His wife came into town the next week. She wore bright colors but was silent; she let her dresses do the talking, my mother averred, and they said she had no taste. I used to see her, tall and dark-haired and thin-lipped, her hems dragging behind her like they carried lead weights, walking alongside the sycamore trees that lined the lower main street. She was as pale as aged ivory, and had faint yellowish shadows under her eyes. I liked to imagine she had some mysterious bodily affliction, or a dark secret wrapped up in a corner of her past. I longed to be of age so that I too might have such a tragedy: it gave one's pace dignity, and lent prominence to the cheekbones. Charpantier's wife seldom talked and she never smiled, and her two small boys were washed-out and listless, and trailed in her wake, whinnying, cast adrift amidst the long eddying shadows of the trees.

They lived in an oversized, blue-gray house on the top of Prospect Hill, the same street my family lived on. The house was surprisingly fanciful for such a man as Charpantier. Its shutters were carved with a frieze of classical figures, its doorknocker was a wooden pelican with a brass bill, and atop its roof, was an eight-sided windowed copula that, if placed squarely on a town green, would have been big enough to host a brass band. Charpantier had a steep, cast-iron bathtub installed within it. When the tub was delivered, it sat in the roadside for an hour like a displaced monument because it proved too heavy for the pair of workmen to lift. The week thereafter, it was all anyone talked about when the name Charpantier was mentioned. Balthezar sidled up to him at work, chortled knowingly, and dropped a casual reference to the *Death of Marat.* Charpantier looked at him steadily and said nothing. Balthezar explained himself, posed no doubt as gracefully as fencing master as he discoursed, detailing the story of the revolutionary and the knife-wielding maiden from Normandy. Charpantier's eyes rested on him the whole time, expressionless.

"Ain't too many maidens from Normandy in Saint-Baptiste, son," he said, and immediately assigned Balthezar to street-crossing duty for the week.

Aggrieved, but with a brave smile, Balthezar told my mother of the conversational misadventure that brought him to be standing with a STOP sign like on oversized lollipop on the town's biggest intersection, which was still never very busy. My mother was heading towards upper main street, on her way to fetch some groceries, and she had me with her by the hand. Balthezar shook his head and lamented the low fortune classical learning had fallen to in a world such as ours. My mother commiserated. That was all he seemed to require, and was able to accept, and he gave a slight bow as we moved on. I looked back at him as he stood there in the middle of the road, sustaining himself against the noonday heat, refusing to relax his posture even an inch. Only after we were halfway down the road did he relent, slump down, and wipe the sweat from his brow.

My mother and I had stopped before the grocer's stand, and I looked back and saw the handkerchief's flash of white, like a surrender. I narrated his actions while my mother scrutinized the shop baskets, and we both breathed in the smell of soft fruit that had been left out all morning in the heat. She was rolling a freestone peach around the palm of her hand, examining it for ripeness, when she finally spoke. "Gallantry implies defeat," she said.

Charpantier's bathtub remained the talk of the town, and entered, I suspect, into many of its dreams. It became Charpantier's habit to bath in the pearly hours of the morning, under an unshaded yellow light. If you looked up at the copula in such an hour, you would see just his head, suspended in the square of window as if it were floating there alone upon the bath water, and looking out over the town it governed. The image was imprinted on our minds like an emblem, the eyes all-seen and all-seeing; and if the town had issued its own currency, that would have been the motif stamped across its back.

On that Wednesday, the day of First Communion, and the ambush and slaughter of the outlaws, Charpantier's head was not visible. The light in the copula was burning, and made a eight-sided box of yellow in the cold gray of the early morning sky. Poirier the baker was preparing a batch of cakes for the First Communion. His shop was three streets below Charpantier's house, which faced him down like an ocean liner at anchor. Every so often, Poirier looked up into the copula window as he worked. Afterwards, he said felt as if he was witnessing an eclipse of the sun, and beholding the sky emptied of what it was ordained to contain. He felt uneasy, although he also admitted he had downed a greasy plateful of leftover sausage and peppers upon waking, and that could well account for his distress and confusion that morning.

He stirred in a spoonful of vanilla extract when he meant to use almond, beat confectioner's sugar into the cake batter instead of granulated, and had to make the buttercream fondant all over again. The mishaps troubled him. The last time a cake of his had failed was the sunny mid-winter morning his mother had woken but declined to go on living, and the gummy richness of a baking fiasco carried for him the taste of death. He read augurs in discarded batter the way old lady Favereau read tea leaves and tarot cards on a carnival day, a bandanna loosely wrapped about her head. That Wednesday morning, Poirier felt with a chill in his belly and an ache in his skull, but he had three different orders of cake to prepare, with a further instruction to pipe an inscription in extra-dark icing, in honor of the Lt. Governor. He went on mixing and measuring in the cold flat light.

He was not the only resident of the town at work so early that morning; for veils had been stitched, flower pots dragged out of position, and guns brought in by stealth.

And Poirier was not the only one to remark upon Charpantier's absences, and whereabouts, so early that morning.

Father Ducie had headed over to the church early, to see that all was in order and the hosts were in proper supply. He had just directed the altar boy, the oldest Beaufils son, to set up a few folding tables in back of the church, for refreshments, when he saw Charpantier drive by. It was not yet six, and the sun was still dim and uncertain. Charpantier's lips were set in a firm little line, Father Ducie said, and his face was encased behind the windshield like an object mounted for display. Father Ducie watched as the sheriff's car went around the corner. He was at the time standing in the front doorway of the church, rubbing his wrists. He noticed a spot of grease on his sleeve, and realized he would have to change his cassock. A patch of light was growing behind the dark lacy heights of an elm, and Father Ducie looked into the brightening sky and thought that, yes, the day would be fair. Just then, an assistant from the Lt. Governor's staff appeared before him.

"He must have walked on the grass because I didn't hear any footsteps," Father Ducie told the papers later that day, "and when I looked down and saw him, I admit I was startled."

The assistant had a light, round face that glowed faintly, like a globe of a streetlight at dusk, above his stiff, dark suit. He introduced himself as "Ray Simone, the Lt. Governor's attaché," and proffered, briefly, to Father Ducie, a pale hand as cool and compact as an unopened lily. He carried his twenty-six years about him like a challenge he had risen to; he carried this paltry burden aloft with widened shoulders, and he folded his face into a frown of deep seriousness whenever he remembered to, which according to Father Ducie, was often.

He frowned, for instance, as he looked out over the small green lawn beside the Church of the Sacred Heart.

An apparent trainee in the business of wearing dark glasses (a business of which the Lt. Governor was master), the assistant drew them away from his eyes whenever he spoke. He asked Father Ducie if he might move the pots of blue hydrangeas from their station by the statue of John the Baptist. He said the Lt. Governor wished to be photographed standing beside the town's name-saint, shoulder to shoulder. (They would be looking in opposite directions, as St John's eyes of stone stared permanently off towards the sea, while the Lt. Governor would no doubt be facing the camera square on.) Father Ducie agreed with a nod, and the assistant, eyes again obscured by his sunglasses, set about dragging the flower pots out of view.

"Perhaps some other citizens will be photographed here today," he remarked. Father Ducie remembered him saying this, and Ray Simone admitted it, but denied any hidden, particular meaning, and maintained he was merely pointing out the place by the statue of St John was ideal for any official snapshot. Nonetheless, the statement was taken up as proof positive that the Lt. Governor knew what was in the works, and had finagled to reap political bounty by associating himself with the ambush. But since he was finished speaking for the time, the assistant had already pushed his sunglasses back up, and his expression was impossible for Father Ducie to read.

Charpantier had apparently headed into the series of small roads that lay in back of the church, overlooking the still backwater. He was spotted by Théramène's younger brother Thésée, who worked an early morning shift in the gas station. Thésée watched from the attached shed while Charpantier parked the police car in front of the pump, and called out for a dollar worth of gasoline. Then he maneuvered his belly out of the car, crossed the street, and headed up the stairs into the town's only rooming house, an oversized gray house with narrow windows, shuttered against the sun like sleeping eyes.

That was where the Lt. Governor and his staff had turned up the day before, in a trio of long black cars that were swift and silent, and had the tops down even though a light rain was falling, like a veil fashioned out of mist. One of their party was said to be Danny Brunet, an ex-vaudevillian film comic of middling fame and shuffling gait. During an election year, the Lt. Governor availed himself of Brunet for public appearances in the Catholic towns south of Shreveport.

Iphigénie, who had been sent out to fetch a quart of milk, said the cars had passed her as she walked home, and the people in them seemed to be carrying their faces unnaturally high. They sat up in the rain as if they could not bother to disdain it and were indifferent to its touch, "like men already drenched," Iphigénie said, "or dead." But everyone knew she was a spooky child, prone to macabre fantasies and unseemly imaginings. No one else had caught a glimpse of Danny Brunet, until Mr LaFarge delivered an order of groceries to the rooming house late that afternoon, and the dining room door swung open. He was sure he spied Brunet's face floating there, long and soft-looking and hook-chinned, like a crescent moon made out of marshmallow.

LaFarge told his wife that the face wasn't like what he thought it would be; it struck him as knowing and lost-looking all at the same time, like a punchline that had got separated from its set-up. "Perhaps he needs an audience just to feel at home with himself," Mr LaFarge said. Then somebody came in and ordered a pound and a half of lard, and his musings on spectacle and identity were curtailed.

It did not take long for Charpantier to emerge from the boarding house the morning of the First Communion. According to Thésée, who kept his eye on the boarding house door, hoping for a glimpse of Brunet (Thésée himself was no particular fan, he admitted, but a star is a star), it was no more than ten minutes before Charpantier re-appeared on the front steps. When he reached his car, he looked at Thésée and grinned.

"Looks like the town's troubles'll be over, boy," Charpantier said, "or leastways the troublemakers." Then he got into the car, wedged his belly into place, slammed the door twice for good measure, and drove off. Thésée stood and watched. It was a new vista of Charpantier's head behind glass, this time in transit not situ, and it had him transfixed.

So by six thirty or so that morning, Thésée had gathered Charpantier planned to take action against some miscreants, although, as soon emerged, he thought Charpantier was referring to a band of gypsies who had been reported drifting from town to town, swiping laundry from the clotheslines, chickens from the coops, and petunias from the graves. Ten minutes later, Théramène pulled into the gas station to get the oil on his father's sedan checked, and pick up a box of jordan almonds for Iphigénie on her First Communion. At the candy counter just inside the station shed, Thésée advised him on a ribbon for the box. He recommended pink, at which point Théramène looked him dead in the eye and said, "Yellow." As Thésée wrapped the box of candy, he mentioned Charpantier had been by. He jutted his chin in the direction of the boarding house, then went silent; struggling on the hook, so to speak, Théramène had to ask what Charpantier had said, and Thésée told him. He added that the dead will surely rest quiet now. Théramène smiled and swatted him around the head, and said, little brother, they already do, it's the ones left behind that set up a squawk.

Théramène could at last afford to be generous and of good humor, for he knew something Thésée did not. The night before, over on the east side of town, and by the light of a passing automobile, Théramène had caught sight of Cammie. He was been on foot, taking the back roads home, and was heading across an alfalfa field gone blue in the shadows of early night. He looked up and found he had walked into some kind of reunion, it seemed like, faces white and flitting by in the dark like moths gathering around a naked light bulb. He saw Cammie, her face showing in the sudden gleam of a passing headlight as if she had been splashed with white oil. He walked faster, averted his eyes, and pulled his collar up to the tips of his ears. He felt like he was crossing through a field of ghosts, the faces were so fair and fugitive, just floating in front of him, bobbing up here and there. No one said anything to him, except one disembodied voice that offered him a piece of sweet potato pie, which somebody else's white hand was holding out on a plate. "For sure, they were outlaws," Théramène remarked to me years afterwards in his dentist's office, "but they did have good country manners."

At Thésée's account of the sheriff and his remark that morning of the First Communion, Théramène raised an eyebrow, though, as he had only a single large one that stretched haphazardly across the bridge of his nose, the effect was probably more ridiculous than knowing. He told Thésée flatly that "troublemakers" could have only meant the outlaw couple.

By early that morning, then, the Camus brothers had more or less caught the right scent; and the Lt. Governor must have known, too, as well as, of course, Charpantier. Throughout that morning, the knowledge entered the town like a quantity of blood trickled, drop by drop, into a pitcher of water. Those who knew proceeded in the next few hours to tell others of what they knew, and that knowledge alternately enticed and repulsed those who bore it.

Some would insist that the plan was, and had always been, simply a call to surrender: the outlaws's car would be forced to a halt, and there would be a peaceful settlement under the broad shade of an ancient oak, by which the man would be arrested, and would accept it, and the woman most likely set free.

Balthezar up to that last believed that this was the intent. He envisioned Lloyd Cannon and himself, in an encounter as rife with etiquette as a sarabande. When the deal was done, each realizing that they were not so very different from the other. Balthezar would extract a silver dollar from his pocket to toss it in the magnolia-scented air, and demonstrate that they were in fact flip sides to the same coin. Wordly and knowing would be their exchanged smiles, and their shared ruefulness a mark of their complicity in the irony of life. Balthezar scribbled notes in the margins of his police report, and they suggested the sensibility with which he proceeded. By the first mention of the outlaws's names, he penned, carefully, in brown ink, "*Nous sommes des honnetes contrabandiers*'- Dumas"; by Father Ducie's account of the First Communion ceremony that morning, a hasty scrawl in blue, that appeared less faded and was a more recent addition: "'I couldn't let them shoot you down like that, Rocky.' Pat O'Brien."

Furthermore, in later years, Balthezar took to making lengthy allusions, delivered with the easy and implied authority of an extract, to a memoir he was planning to write, but in the event, never got around to beginning. His approach, you could gather, was distinct from Théramène's, who was an amateur historian informed by the rules of science. Balthezar sought not to transcribe events objectively, but, rather, to deliver the considerations of a strategist of human affairs, and of a connoisseur of all matters ethical, tactical, and ceremonial. For him, it was clear that the treachery was Sheriff Charpantier's; and that the target of his deceit was not the outlaws, but himself, Balthezar. The understandings that he had worked to come to with the outlaws and their people, Charpantier had gone and twisted to his own bloody, and completely unsubtle, ends. In Balthezar's book, Charpantier's transgression was not so much legal, procedural, or ethical, but, greater than all these, aesthetic; and while Balthezar was in no doubt that the matter was a tragedy, he was equally in no doubt that he was its hero.

Around quarter to seven the morning of the First Communion, the dressmaker Henriette Grenier came to deliver Perpetuée's Communion veil to the LaFarge house. As she looked out the window of Perpetuée's bedroom, she saw a stack of rifles leaned up against a side door. She blinked, and when she looked again, they were gone. She half-wondered if she had imagined the sight (though in few hours, it was clear she had not); then Perpetuée called loudly for attention and compliments, as she had put on the veil and was attempting unsuccessfully to view her reflection in the window.

The veil was as heavy and richly embroidered as a bride's, with figures of fleurs-de-lis scattered through the fine net backwork. As Mrs. LaFarge had insisted, with less than a day to spare, the veil was pieced in with another so that it fell not just to Perpetuée's shoulders, but an inch or two below her knees. When Henriette turned to look at the girl, she felt for an instant she had caught sight of a ghost, and she shivered, and blessed herself. "That girl is as fat as a suckling pig," Henriette was quoted in Balthezar's report of the day's incident, "and far too young for a design of such intricacy, and no it doesn't matter a single bit that her coloring is gorgeous." My mother had given Perpetuée the same compliment one day she had come from school with me; that time, I ran and hid behind the dining room curtains and refused to budge until it was time for supper. But at the reported quote, which Balthezar passed on to my mother after church the next Sunday, I felt vindicated, and eager to be generous to Perpetuée the next time I saw her, and could blurt out the entire, puncturing remark.

Mrs. Roux was also seen walking by LaFarge's around seven that morning; she had her fingers in her mouth, Perpetuée said, who was looking out the window with her First Communion dress half on and half off, and seen her. She was walking very slowly. "Like a woman balancing a heavy basket on her head," Perpetuée said, and when I spoke to her thirty-four years later, she stiffened her neck to demonstrate.

Mrs. Roux, however, would never speak of why she was by LaFarge's that morning, and if she had suspected what lay in wait for her daughter behind the sweet mock-orange. Years later, I asked her how it was that Cammie had happened to visit her just the night before. "Leave it, sister," she said to me. It was the only time during our conversation that she looked at me. "What's dead is dead." Her voice was as slack and toneless as the muscles of her bare calves. She was sitting on her front porch in a faded print shift, shelling a bowl of snow peas, when I turned up, unbidden, as the sun was setting. She went back to them, as if I weren't there, and in a twinkling, I was not. When I'd reached the far end of the swept yard, already shadowed by night, she called out, "The way I look at it, my girl died the day she took up with that fella."

By eight o'clock on the morning on which the outlaws were to be slaughtered, Balthezar was in the vicinity of the church, though he did not see Charpantier, and indeed, he looked a little surprised when Father Ducie hailed him from the church doorway, and mentioned that Charpantier had driven by earlier. Father Ducie said he himself was waiting for the First Communion flowers to be delivered. Balthezar lowered his eyelids and nodded as though a grave confidence had been shared, and he breathed in the scent of the potted lilies stationed on either side of the door. He was in the habit of stopping by church to say a rosary two or three mornings a week, but, in light of the sacrament due to be performed, he had foregone observance that morning. He stood there, as upright as a military commander on point of accepting his enemy's surrender, and hesitated a second as though being briefed by an invisible translator by his ear. Rather than smile and say goodbye, he bowed stiffly from the neck, and moved on.

Thésée, who was at that moment in the gas station shed, and just getting around to putting back the colored ribbons he had brought down for his brother, saw him next. Balthezar was walking slowly along the street, thinking something. He wiped his hands once or twice against his trouser legs, a gesture which Thésée noted because he thought it meant that Balthezar was nervous, and contemplating his impending rendezvous with the outlaws. Balthezar headed over to the shack, and bought a bottle of raspberry lemonade. "Busy day," Thésée said, his right hand tangled up in a length of lavender ribbon. Balthezar raised the bottle of lemonade to his temple, saluted with it, and said with a solemn, gently chiding smile, that a First Communion day was not so much busy as significant.

"I was talking about for you officers of the law," Thésée said, and went on to repeat the gist of his conversation with Théramène.

Balthezar stood there still holding the bottle of lemonade out in mid-air, and listened. But all he heard was what he already knew, that the outlaws were in the vicinity, and were to be dealt with soon, and though he was perhaps momentarily troubled that anyone outside the force of law knew that much, the matter appeared to fade from his mind. He had no inkling of bloodshed when, a few minutes later, he wandered off.

But that inkling was already seeping into the consciousness of the town. Henriette Grenier was to claim that when she left the LaFarge house that morning, she felt a chill surround her, despite the sunlight. She walked down the sidewalk, placing her feet with precision and forethought, so that like a superstitious child, she avoided stepping on the cracks. As she passed the corner of the superette, she heard men's voices. At first she could not tell where they were coming from, and she told Balthezar they struck her as disembodied but not displaced. "It was like hearing somebody's ghost in the room where they've died, rustling around the ceiling like a pigeon trapped in the rafters," she said, and Balthezar dutifully penned the remark into his report.

She looked into the blue sky that May morning, shielding her eyes with one hand. She watched a bluebird circle high in the air, and descend as if pulled by a string into the rustling yellow-green leaves. Immediately, a rifle barrel jutted above the bushes; then just as sharply it was jerked away, and Henriette heard issued a gruff admonition to hold fire. Not sparing a minute to bless herself a second time that morning, she hurried on into the main street of the town.

By Beau Geste, the hairdresser's, she stopped to look in the window and adjust her hat. She glimpsed the reflection of Louis Sante next to her own. He had a gun in his belt, she said, which caught the sunlight. He was there but for the twinkling of an eye, she said, for, by the time she turned to him, he was gone. Some doubted if she had seen him at all, but she did recall, with a seamstress's precision, the color and cut of his denims.

As she looked down the road, she saw Théramène approaching. He was on his way again to LaFarge's superette. At first, when questioned by the newspapers, he said he was going there to look for a small toy to go with the candy for his sister; but later, he admitted he was really hoping to catch a glimpse of Danny Brunet or at least the Lt. Governor, as they headed down the main street towards the Church of the Sacred Heart. With that mind, he planned on malingering by the magazine rack until the church bells rang, and called the town and its celebrity guests to the First Communion.

Henriette Grenier stopped and stood on the street corner. She called out to Théramène to be careful, there were armed men hiding out. Théramène took her to mean a single armed man, which he understood to be Lloyd Cannon. His heart rose at the prospect, Théramène said, for Lloyd Cannon was altogether more exciting a personage, and, he was bound to say, historically significant, than either the Lt. Governor or Danny Brunet. He was not afraid, for Cannon had never proved a threat to ordinary folks such as himself. "It would be like seeing an animal in its natural habitat, which for him would be on the run," Théramène told the papers. So Théramène thanked Henriette, and stepped off the curb, unperturbed, and almost exhilarated. "I thought if I saw him I would tell him how he and his gal had met my sister Iphigénie," he said, "and how she was taken with them, and maybe get them to sign the box of candy for her. That would have made her First Communion complete." As he passed along the street, he watched a flock of sparrows rise from a boxwood hedge, twittering, in a spiral, like a handful of ashes tossed into a wind. Their wings turned silver and gold when they caught the light. He guessed it was sometime around eight o'clock, because when he looked down the road, he saw Albert Brossette, the postman, slinging his heavy mailbag over his shoulder as he began his morning route. Albert was whistling, and to Théramène, it was like hearing the sound of a cock's crow, but for the first or second time that day, he wasn't sure.

It was also coming up to eight when LaFarge looked up at his clock and the chimes on his shop door rattled. A man stepped up to the counter and ordered three packs of Lucky Strikes, and a half dozen sandwiches. He had black stubble on his face, his accent was positively nasal, and, to LaFarge's ears, stank of the north. LaFarge was sure he had never seen him before. Which kind of sandwiches'll it be, LaFarge asked, and the man said it didn't matter. What can a man be doing, LaFarge almost asked, that he don't care what food he puts in his belly; but the man was a stranger, and seemed to want it to stay that way, with his eyes cast down, and his mouth following suit. When the man reached for his wallet, LaFarge thought he saw a flash of metal, but the man's jacket quickly fell back into place, and LaFarge could not be sure. What was truly unsettling, the man left without waiting for his change. LaFarge called out to him, but the man kept going, swift as a shadow and as featureless, without a backward glance. LaFarge felt rebuffed and ridiculous. When he had regained himself, a shiver of trepidation came over him.

"It crossed my mind that he was part of some criminal gang planning to rob the local bank," LaFarge later told the paper. As soon as the door had swung closed, he went over to it and lowered the shade, and was suddenly grateful he had never had cause to open a bank account in all his life. A sense of his fiscal improvidence settled on his shoulders, he said, "like a blessing from on high," and his spirits lifted. Then Perpetuée emerged from the backstairs entrance, her veil hanging so heavy on the back of her head that her chin was drawn up and her throat exposed like a warbling choir singer's. She roamed among the racks of baked goods, and practiced her stately First Communion walk, while LaFarge watched, and clapped his hands in time, and told her she was as elegant as an infanta of old.

LaFarge was not the only proprietor who found himself dealing with the demands of an out-of-towner's belly that morning. Around the time that LaFarge was standing in the shadows of his doorway, rejoicing in his own insolvency, Octave Dubru, the rooming house owner, was in his kitchen, frying up eggs and bacon for the Lt. Governor and Danny Brunet. Octave always liked to have the kitchen spic and span by eight every morning, but on this day, he had made an exception.

Octave knew that his wife would never have honored the Lt Governor's breakfast order, because solid food was prohibited before Communion. He had urged her to stay in bed, and through his own efforts, saw to it that his two guests of state-wide renown had their breakfast in relative secret, so they would still be able to partake of the Eucharist later that day. The sheriff had stopped earlier by that morning, and Octave thought another place would have to be set, but Charpantier left after five or ten minutes. Octave had heard them all laughing, darkly, and too loudly, as if to impress each other in the face of a dirty joke. It was not the kind of laughter he associated with the mild-mannered, sad-faced comedian, and Octave speculated and brooded over what the joke must have been. But the bacon began to sputter, and he soon forgot about them.

The smell of the bacon drifted upstairs to Mrs. Dubru's bedroom; and to her, the day was always a simple and profound case of sacrilege. The bacon smell hit her like a slap in the face, she told my mother. As she lay there, she envisioned a lump of animal flesh sitting next to a consecrated host, deep in the Lt. Governor's belly, as though she had a cutaway view of his insides. In her estimation, the Lord did what was necessary to prevent such a convergence coming to pass that day. At the time, however, the very vision turned her stomach, and only after a two day's hot-water-and-lemon-juice fast did she allow Octave to bring her a tray of buttered toast and black coffee again in the morning.

Honore Dubru, Octave's younger brother, was already out on the streets that morning, talking his exercise before the day grew hot, and the commotion from the First Communion crowded the sidewalks. Whenever he ventured into the town, Honore wore a suit of spotless, starched white linen. Octave had insisted he dress that way, since his eighteenth birthday, to master, and to demonstrate he had mastered, cups of tea and coffee and red wine, and the vagaries of mud and dust upon the road. When he was eight years old, Honore had stared straight into an eclipse of the sun, and the next morning, he arose from bed, well-rested, ravenous, and stone-cold blind. When he was abroad in the town, a lean, uncrumpled and vaguely luminous figure, Honore could be heard tapping his way, sometimes lightly, sometimes insistently. He was always immaculate, and he usually paused to nod at passers-by, and exchange pleasantries of the day. He was skilled at recognizing people too, by the heaviness of their tread, or the scent that they carried: violet water, chalk dust or pouch tobacco; horse feed, ground cinnamon, or gasoline.

"The smell of bacon was already thick in the air when I set out," Honore said in newspaper reports from the time. Within a few hours of the arrival of the Lt. Governor and his entourage, Honore developed a distaste for the sound of Lt. Governor's voice, which he now associated with the greasy smoke of bacon, and the clatter of pans as Octave clumsily manned the stove. The Lt. Governor sounded as rough as cheap whiskey, Honore said, and smelled like it too; and as for Brunet, Honore concluded he belonged back in the silents, for his voice was as thin and wispy as a fume of paint, eternally on the point of evaporating.

As Honore walked down the sidewalk the morning of the First Communion, he encountered Sophia. He was heading in the direction of LaFarge's, and he guessed she was going towards the church. "I knew her by the sound of her heels," he said, "quick, and small, and clickety, and as I got closer I could smell the flowers she was carrying. She was in no mood for small talk, however, and I merely nodded as I passed." He proceeded a few hundred yards down the sidewalk, and there, he said, he smelled gunpowder and hot metal.

This point was disputed by everyone else, for no one had heard a gun go off so early that morning. But at the cross-questioning, Honore's mouth first wobbled like an old dog's on a hot day, then it firmed up. He became specific, and even clearer in his enunciation, as though he were talking to idiots. "I was standing at that point in the sidewalk where the sycamore root erupts from under the cement. My cane finds the spot, and there, as is my habit, I rested a moment. I took out a handkerchief and wiped my brow, and I smelled hot metal, and a tinge of smoke. Also, I heard some creatures rustling in the hedge alongside the sidewalk. They were heavier and less agile than a squirrel or a pigeon, or some such." He did not call out, he said, because he feared being ignored, and that fear impinged upon his dignity in a way that blindness never could. His face was difficult to read. He wore shaded glasses, not with black lenses as favored by the Lt. Governor; but green, as if they were made of tempered crème de menthe. Balthezar took his statement and thanked him for his precision. Clearly, disability has its compensations, he commented, and so noted down; but his report neglected to record Honore's response.

Poirier passed by Honore too; he was delivering the first installment of cakes for the First Communion. He had one large, square cake, decorated for the Lt. Governor in an unpalatable blue which disheartened him just to look at. In addition, he brought along a batch of small hazelnut meringues iced with coffee-praline, a combination which he felt was too sophisticated for the gathering, but made anyway, in homage to his own good taste. He wished Honore good day, loudly, and from a fair distance, so as not to startle him, and he hurried along, the tray balanced upon his left shoulder. "The only thing I smelled at that moment was vanilla sugar," Poirier said. "And I was in a hurry to get the first batch of cakes set up, so I could bring on the second."

Around this time, the Lt. Governor was wiping the grease from his lips, and removing himself from the breakfast table. One of his men had already brought the car around to the front, and it sat there, gleaming and black, while the Lt. Governor licked the fingers of one hand, and fastened the middle button of his suit coat with the other. Summoned by the smell of the bacon, Mrs. Dubru came downstairs. She admitted later she was ready to have a sharp word with her husband, for the good of both their souls, but because the Lt. Governor was still there, along with the minor movie star, she reined her temper in, and said good morning. It was not entirely clear where the Lt. Governor was headed at that point. Danny Brunet was staying behind, and in the aftermath, some took that to mean the Lt. Governor was going out on some matter of state business: that is, he was heading to the planned site of the capture, or shooting, of the outlaws. His driver let it drop that the Lt. Governor at the very least knew that the outlaws were in the area. The eventual and official word from his spokesman was that the Lt. Governor wished to go by the Church of the Sacred Heart before the First Communion, for a moment of quiet prayer, and apparently a few photos as well, for a cameraman was part of his entourage that morning.

According to Mrs. Dubru, the comedian looked grim-faced, "the way those people always do in their off hours. He gave the Lt. Governor a brief wave, but that one wasn't looking." He had already set off down the broad front steps of the rooming house. No one in the rooming house actually watched the car move off, or noticed what road it took. We all heard, however, of where it wound up.

The driver that day was Luke Simone, the brother of the self-proclaimed "governor's attaché." Luke had the same high, pearly forehead as Ray, and the same hard-eyed impatience of the unduly confident. He was obviously unfamiliar with the roads of Saint-Baptiste, but that proved no impediment to the speed he exercised upon them. He neglected to take the immediate right, which was marked by a cleft stump of an oak, and led directly to the town's main road. Instead he took the second turn. For the first twenty miles this route ran parallel to the main one, and was cordoned off from it by a thick line of trees. The road started off wide and even, but it led into the woods and soon petered out to a dirt road, then a walking trail established in the time of the Indians, and finally nothing at all. Luke Simone had set them on the course of casual disaster.

The Lt. Governor, installed in the back of the car, was still groggy with sleep, and almost stupefied by the fat from his breakfast. Luke Simone was eventually interviewed by Claude Barbier; though never published, a fragment of the encounter was filed with Barbier's papers in the local library. Luke said he looked in his rear view mirror and watched the Lt. Governor in his dark glasses, smacking his lips several times, as if to free bits of food from between his teeth. The photographer, a spare, dapper sort of fellow, whose name has been lost to the record, made attempts at small talk, Luke said, but the Lt. Governor only grunted in reply, and once or twice took another nip from his pocket flask.

When they had driven a few miles down the road, and passed nothing but trees, it occurred to Luke he must have taken a wrong turn. Instead of first clearing the slope that rose before them, Luke put the car into reverse, and began a U-turn. Too late, he heard the gears of a heavy goods vehicle, and found himself facing into the oncoming front fender of a lumber truck. Hidden as the Lt. Governor's car was by the rise of the hill, the lumber truck proceeded at full throttle. At the crest of the hill, it stopped a moment, poised, and that was when the truck's driver saw them, and his mouth dropped open. The truck rolled heavily down the slope towards the Lt. Governor's car. It veered to the left, and left the road entirely, but not before the front of the truck caught the back of the Lt. Governor's car, gave it one almighty shove and sent it into a half tailspin.

"I heard the brakes screech, and glass shatter. I felt speed gathering pace, and gravity giving way, and it was heart-stopping, and the most exciting moment of my life, because I realized there was nothing I could do." Luke's words were recorded, in Barbier's rounded script, where whole words were joined up as one, as if they were caught up in the moment themselves.

Luke Simone found he was not hurt, and he was just turning around to enquire after the two men in back, when he saw the truck driver had already stepped out of the cab and was coming towards them. Luke noticed the man's eyes were fixed on the back seat. It looked as if the Lt. Governor had been thrown forward, and hit his head, for he was unconscious, and his dark glasses were askew. "I was ashamed to see him like that," Luke told Claude, "so I quickly looked away."

Then Luke Simone and the photographer hurried out of the car. They heaved the body of the Lt. Governor out of the back seat, and laid him by the side of the road. Amidst the fresh air, the timothy grass, and the hovering butterflies, the Lt. Governor took up space like a disused ice box, while the three men looked at each other, and wondered what to do next.

Luke told Claude Barbier he feared the outlaws might come upon them in this deserted wood at any moment, and the thought of it made him shudder. "It was not the fear of physical injury, but the loss of face." There was a camera on hand, Luke Simone had remembered, and he was certain the outlaws would take pictures of their capture of the state's second highest official, and send evidence of the humiliation far and wide. Of course, everyone knew the pair were at large and in the vicinity, Luke Simone added, with no apparent prompting from Claude; Claude circled the remark and affixed a question mark above it, high and round as the crayoned sun in a first grader's picture of creation. "Just then," Claude Barbier wrote, "Luke Simone was more transfixed by the threat of humiliation than bloodshed, for he had never faced down the barrel of a firearm."

As the Lt. Governor lay there under the warm spring sunlight, Luke thought he saw the eyelids flicker. He was about to step in, and draw his face closer to the Lt. Governor's for a more definitive look, when Balthezar Broudreau emerged from the trees.

"He was slight and light-colored, and moved at a slant against the height and dark of the trees," Luke Simone said. "At first I thought it was a child who had wandered into the woods, but then he came closer and his badge flashed in the sunlight, and I realized he was a policeman." Balthezar had been patrolling the main street just beyond the gray-green line of cypress, finishing his lemonade, when he heard the crash, and he came forward to help, and to officiate. He commented on his own actions in a letter that ran weeks later in the *Gazette*: "This incident serves to illustrate a conclusion I had reached some time ago: namely, that upholding the honor of law in all situations is as crucial as delivering any practical service – more so, for such honor is the source from which all civil authority emanates. For the officer of the state, therefore, dignity is no luxury."

True to the precepts of his political philosophy, the first thing Balthezar did was to lean over the body of the Lt. Governor, and straighten his dark glasses. Then he directed Luke Simone to help him stand the Lt. Governor up. Luke said later he had no idea what Balthezar had in mind, but it was not his to question. Balthezar clasped the Lt. Governor under the arms, and Luke held him around the knees, and the Lt. Governor was standing. "He was the highest official present, and he needs be presided over this matter of state which was unfolding beneath his gaze, albeit unconscious," Balthezar wrote. Balthezar took to prefacing his subsequent remarks on the subject with phrases like "as I have written before," and "in my previous communication to the public." To Balthezar Broudreau, his letter to the editor had straightaway taken on the status of a set text routinely assigned in the school of life.

Straining a bit under the weight of the Lt. Governor that fine May morning, Balthezar took command. He directed the photographer to take notes, while he questioned the truck driver and Luke. He ascertained the speed and direction of the lumber truck, and established who was responsible for what. When the questioning was completed, the photographer slipped the notepad into Balthezar's shirt pocket. All three then heaved the Lt.

Governor's body back into the backseat of the car. Balthezar sniffed the Lt. Governor's lips. He told them to see the Lt. Governor received appropriate care, though from his experience, he guessed the condition was not too serious. The photographer laughed, and said as long as nobody light a match thereabouts. Balthezar frowned, for, as he told my mother, he felt as though his own dignity had been impugned. Then he strolled back to the station to file the paperwork. The activity of dotting the i's and crossing the t's, in the literal sense, closed the matter for him, and filled him with contentment. He looked at the finished file, he said, and smiled with satisfaction. Charpantier, who had the story from Balthezar by then, was at his own desk, and he smiled back, for his morning had been fruitful, too.

*   *   *

There were nineteen brides and grooms of Christ, that morning, arrayed in white and cream and ivory. The girls wore sashes and hair ribbons that were tinted, like party favors at a wedding, the colors of jordan almonds, pale pink, powder blue, lilac and primrose yellow, except for the Nadal girl who stuck out like a sore thumb in a moss green tissue faille, with a stiff black velvet sash that jutted out a half foot on either side.

The Nadals always were contrary, my mother said. Mrs. Nadal told her a few weeks before that they'd gotten the idea for Arlette's dress from a fashion magazine - as if that was a recommendation - and that in both New York and Paris that season, moss green and black were all the rage. "But for a girl's First Holy Communion?" my mother could not help asking, her hands held out momentarily, beseeching Mrs. Nadal to regain order and balance. No one had to be a slave to white, my mother hastened to point out, for her own daughter's dress was to be pale blue: distinctive, but tasteful, and long identified as the color of the mother of God. But Mrs. Nadal only lifted the corners of mouth slightly, in that absent and superior way she had, and inquired as to the takings for the Guild of Assisi recent book drive. Fashion is not style, my mother declared firmly as she recounted the tale later that summer, and she set the pitcher of lemonade down so heavily, to punctuate her point, that the slices of lemon were startled and jumped up in a circle inside the frosted glass. Balthezar, who was sitting with us on our porch, smiled from the depths of the rocking chair with self-satisfaction, like a schoolmaster who has done his job well.

My mother had always maintained, and I remember this axiom as well as I do the envoi to her favorite Ave Marie, by Gonoud not Shubert, or her recipe for toffee-almond ice cream sauce, that, except for black, and shades of blue, the hardest color to match exactly is white. In retrospect the whites and creams and ivories in the church that Wednesday proved her point. As my mother recalled, when she ran to the church that morning just after the outlaws had been blasted to bits, her kitchen towel still trailing from her hands, she could not help but notice it: some of the First Communicants were in cloth so white it had a blue undertone like snow, but others were in a white warmed with a tone of peach or vanilla or winter wheat; or ivory, as if the fabric had collected age into its folds, and taken on the very tint of time; or dove grey, like something eternally beneath the shadow of a rain cloud.

And the whiteness had a range of textures within it too: pique and sateen and seersucker and tulle and organza. It was pleated and gathered and pressed and smocked; cuffed and starched and beaded and frilled. The whiteness of the First Communicants was resplendent and manifold. They were like a flock of birds, their feathers shifting shades of white in the sunlight, and the noise of gobbling barely buried in their throats. They spilled out of the church that sunny May morning, intent, like an animal that has caught the scent of blood. They rushed straightway to the car that gleamed the color of desert sands, a throng of flesh and fabric in the raw spring light. Charpantier was standing a few yards from the automobile, and he managed to catch one or two of them on his outstretched arms, and swing them away, but they struggled loose, and joined the ones already mobbing the bullet-slashed Ford.

Iphigénie, small and wiry, had reached the car first. "I always figured she would be front and center at any disaster," my brother Henri said later that week. "It's where she belongs, with those crisscrossed eyes of hers." He had his hands in pockets and was attempting to look old and wise as he gazed out the window, and paced. I thought that he was right, and this so annoyed me that I reached over to the fruit bowl, picked up an orange, and threw it at him. My father, sitting in his armchair in the corner, looked up from his reading, and told me to be careful, I could put someone's eye out. Then, order restored, he turned back to his page in Bowen's *The Tragic Era*.

That day of her First Communion, Iphigénie was wearing a dress of pure white eyelet, with a pair of gloves that clasped at the wrist with a mother of pearl chip. Almost as soon as she ascended the running board of the car, she peeled them off. They eventually fell into the road, where they were trod upon and kicked to the side and were later picked up by an insurance man from Baton Rouge, who had a domed forehead but no neck. He had come to Saint-Baptiste to see the bodies of the slaughtered outlaws, and he eventually snipped the gloves into half-inch squares, and sold them through the classified pages in the Baton Rouge Post as "Genuine Pieces of Cammie Roux's Death Dress." We knew because a week later, Claude Barbier set about purchasing the relic, at the *Gazette*'s expense, and wrote up a story which unmasked the true origins of the item. The first tip-off, he wrote, was the paucity of squares the man had on offer. The insurance man ultimately broke down under Claude's questioning, and admitted to something of a swindle. "But it is Cammie's Roux's blood upon them," the man asserted, as a parting remark in his own defense. "I defy you to prove otherwise."

When Iphigénie jumped up to the running board of the Ford on the morning of her First Communion, she looked into the car, she said, expectant, almost impatient, waiting for something to begin, and not a bit afraid. "It was like a movie," she said afterwards. She was never very clear on what it was that she saw. From where she was standing, she would have been staring directly into what was left of Cammie's face, but she could recall only a series of images that flitted before her, as if they were pulled along by a string then jerked away altogether: a shock of reddish-blond hair, the smell of tuna fish, and a fly buzzing inside the shattered windshield. And she said she suddenly thought of a mouse she'd seen in her momma's pantry one morning that November previous, felled in a trap, its face turned upwards at an unnatural angle, open-mouthed as if astonished, and so very still.

"The young girl had entered into the death scene of criminals most wanted," the story in the *Gazette* pronounced, and in short order, her part in the scene apparently ended. Both feet planted on the running board of the car, her nose a bare inch from where the window glass would have been if it hadn't been blasted out, Iphigénie fainted. So tight was the crush of schoolchildren around her, however, she did not fall over, but remained bolstered upright for the entire spectacle

It was as if they had converged into a single entity, the First Communicants. They rushed around the car, surrounding it on all sides. They had emerged from the church attended by a low buzz carried mostly within themselves, and the sound fell deeper, shifted a gear lower, as they approached the Ford, then plunged their hands through the blasted out windows. "We knew what we were going to do without having to say anything, or even look at each other," Richard Forestier said afterwards.

Their progress was direct, but somehow slowed down, the baker said: "It was like watching something walk underwater, or in a dream." According to my father, the movement was deliberate, on-going, and repetitious-in-the-making. "They proceeded like creatures trapped in the eternal present," he said, and raised his chin significantly, to match the import of his insight. He had always thought grammar held more insights into the human condition than numbers ever could, but there were no solid career opportunities in that direction, and he had to content himself with reading out incidences of split infinitives from the local paper.

Pressed up beside Iphigénie, and taking no notice of her, Marie-Aimée Clement leaned into the smashed-out side window. She was wearing lilac-trimmed georgette with elbow-length leg-o'mutton sleeves. Marie-Aimée plucked at something, and when she had gained it, snapped it in two, and held it aloft: a gold neck chain that caught the May sunlight, and trembled in the air, like a shiver upon your skin. A streak of blood darkened her sleeve. It first it was only a slim arc, but it spread quickly, like a shadow. She was smiling.

Josephina, by now watching the scene from the back window of her dance studio, insisted someone in the crowd burst into applause at that moment, but no one else could recall such a detail, and Father Ducie later intimated from several porches around town that artists, especially of the would-be and free-thinking variety, were subject to such bizarre fancies that they could not fairly be called liars, no, neither in justice nor in mercy, for that would be unkind.

They were gathered around the Ford like gulls settled along a fence top, the First Communicants, posted there but not entirely still, in sunlight that fell so white and dry and fine through the residual gunsmoke that it was like a powder settling. Their elbows flapped every so often, and their heads bobbed up. They did not actually have command of the car for so very long, but every moment that they did seemed attenuated, like the leg muscles of a stalking animal.

In actual fact, the number of minutes totaled less than two and a quarter. This we found out later from Achilles Daudet, who carried his grandfather's aluminum watch in his pocket at all times. He was grateful for any occasion to refer to it, because he could once again tell the story of how his grandfather had spent his youth working in the tin mines of South America, and had been given the choice, as payment for his labor, of a watch of platinum, or aluminum. He chose the latter, and lived to see it become worthless. Few are granted the privilege, Achilles Daudet would say, of witnessing transience so concretely; and he looked thoughtfully into the eyes of his listeners while he spoke, as if he was measuring their profundity by their reaction. In his out-stretched hand, he would turn the watch over and over, letting it collect puddles of light into its many dents; then he slipped the watch into his coat pocket, and waited for his audience to speak. But, and never more than in this instance, that day of the First Communion by the car the color of desert sands, time was felt not so much in its passage of minutes as in its arrest and suspension.

The onlookers faced the car and the First Communicants, and took in an expanse of white and gold and flesh and blood. "It was like being in church, except it held my attention," Octave Dubru told Claude Barbier. Octave had heard the shots, and seen people hurrying along the road beneath his rooming house window in such numbers that they set the kitchen curtains aflutter. He put the dish-washing aside, stood out on the sidewalk, and was swept along to the Church of the Sacred Heart. Eventually his wife joined him, turning up by his side, in a housecoat she held resolutely shut with one clenched hand. When Octave mentioned the Mass in his comment to Claude

Barbier, her gaze upon him hardened, and she switched hands, and blessed herself. Octave tried to take back his words, his voice a rising stutter in Claude's direction, but it was too late.

Claude Barbier had not initially been at the church that day of the First Communion. The assignment he considered so minor and mundane that he handed it on to Joseph Nidier, who was just starting out as a stringer. Joseph had a lock of black hair that perpetually fell in his eyes and gave him an air of poetic uncertainty. "500 words," Claude told Joseph on Tuesday afternoon (Claude's eyes were shut, Joseph recalled years later, his face was set in the direction of the clock on the wall, and he had his feet up on the desk), "remember it's better to leave a detail out than to get it wrong, and be sure to spell everybody's name right."

But at the sound of the gunfire that day, Claude put down the cinnamon fritter he had taken a bite out of. He had only just settled himself down at the café. He gave a fleeting thought to the dining table on the Mary Celeste, found fully set for meal that was never consumed; and, as soon as he ventured out onto the sidewalk, he was caught up in the rush of people swept along in the direction of the Church of the Sacred Heart.

Claude noted down Octave's remark, about Mass not holding his attention, and later admitted in his diary that his heart turned a somersault, rejoicing at the guileless irreverence of the words. When Octave sought to retract them moments afterwards, Claude had already moved off to stand under the shade of an elm tree, where he looked off in the distance, and scribbled down stray thoughts, mostly unrelated to the scene at hand but jogged loose by it, before they escaped him forever.

All the while, the first communicants were picking at the inside of the car. Joseph Nidier stood at the mid-center of the crowd, his notepad two inches from his eyes as he took notes on the children on their First Communion.

Albertine Hubert reached into the front seat of the Ford and snatched a pack of cigarettes. She dropped it, and they spilled out over the road, and tumbled towards Charpantier like a miniature logjam. Brigitte Lerond pulled out a length of green ribbon, and it hung in the air a moment, before she hung it over her shoulders. Then Robert Brinon, a touch of his daddy's hair cream still glistening on the top of his ears, held aloft a frayed patch of hyacinth blue. In the time it takes a shimmer of light to pass along a fold of silk, frays of hyacinth blue bloomed above the wrecked car that was the color of desert sands, like a glade of flowers sprung up in mid-air. Then, as if a breeze had kicked up and brushed them all the other way, there was a scattering of pale green as well.

The hands darted down like sharp-beaked birds from a sky so bright it looked like heated metal. Afterwards some insisted they heard the cawing of birds in the background, a cawing so intense it sprung up and grew like a thick foliage of sound, with stems and leaves, and echoes like vagrant tendrils. Others said that was nonsense, the only sounds were the Ford motor, and a cry from one of the children every so often, and the police calling out orders as they came forward and pulled the children away.

Perpetuée LaFarge had been seated inside the pew by the window in the Church of the Sacred Heart, and among the last of the First Communicants to flee, she was at the back of the swarm. Her veil was so heavy it had fallen off to one side, and she had nearly tripped over it as she made her way down the church steps. Hectore Santiago, running along next to her, actually did stumble over it, and gave it a peevish little tug to help himself up, and she howled as though her scalp were being ripped off, and affixed both hands to her temples. But it made no difference because everyone's attention was focused elsewhere. In the end, Perpetuée gave up, and, her veil trailing lopsidedly behind her, attempted to join her classmates. All the churchgoers had quit the church by then too; but when they got within a few yards of Charpantier, they stopped, and watched, like explorers who have gained sight of an ocean but have no intention of broaching it.

Everyone agreed that Father Ducie was the last to emerge from the church. His top vestment was gold and stiff and shiny in the sun like the foil wrapping on a chocolate Easter bunny. It was slightly askew, and he looked bewildered, my father said; he stood on the bottom step of the church, blinking in the strong light as though he had spent his entire life in a cave. He called out "Children!" at what was apparently the loudest voice he could muster, but it sounded so feeble in the out-of-doors that he resorted to pretending he had not spoken at all, and hurriedly fussed with his collar instead.

"I could not believe what was happening," Father Ducie told Claude Barbier later. "After all, it was the day of their First Communion." He joined the swelling crescent of on-lookers.

Arlette Nadal in her dark green tissue faille was by then moving among the white-clad first communicants like a bassline to a tune, or a catfish at the bottom of a tank, nosing along the edges, the width of her stiff bow keeping everyone away and preventing her from approaching anything, including the bullet-raked Ford. Finally, weary of trying to find an opening beside the car, she plunked herself down on a tree stump, looking, by dint of her dress color, as though she was already perpetually in the shade, and crying because she could not get any closer to the slaughtered outlaws.

The youngest Beaufils boy was plucking at something inside the Ford car. Benedict's light blond hair shone, nearly blinding in the sun, and his white sailor suit fairly shimmered. He nabbed a cologne spritzer, the size of his own fist. One side of the flask had been blasted off to a few ragged points of glass, and each of them caught the sun, like a thing afire. He held the bottle higher, and he must have also grasped tighter, for the broken edges of the glass cut into him. His knuckles were suddenly bright with blood. He jerked his hand sharply towards his face, then away. He flung the flask aside, where it fell into a clump of goldenrod, and he ran, howling, towards the cordon of adults, to his mother, where he made to hide behind her legs. Her knees soon were streaked with blood, along with the hem of her powder blue moiré dress, which she carefully preserved in her back closet that afternoon and never wore again. But the blood was only Benedict's, my brother Henri pointed out, and he did not consider it a worthy memento of the day.

It was as if, with Benedict Beaufils's defection, a seal on a tight jar had been broken. My mother swore she heard a small hiss, but that was no doubt her own sharp release of breath, my father told her, her disbelief springing a leak at last. Charpantier rushed forward, as if freed from some invisible cordon that had been holding him fast. He was galumphing a bit from the heat, and his fat. The officers from the surrounding woods had by now joined him, and they fanned out around him, brown as though formed from sepia light, and casting shadows a shade darker, and both light and shadow were converging upon the children in white.

As the police approached, the First Communicants scattered, fluttered off one by one, to roost in the semicircle of adults. They stood there, holding their mothers's hands, and staring wide-eyed and vaguely accusatory, as if seeking protection from the spectacle they had just been devouring, and of which they had been part.

All the First Communicants had scattered, except for Iphigénie, who, at the peremptory departure of Marie-Aimée, slumped down on the running board like a half-full bag of laundry. At that sight, the crowd was still for a moment, until it was clear, when one of the officers grabbed at her wrist and felt her pulse, that the girl had only fainted. The crowd loosened up as though a reprieve had arrived. They stretched their necks a bit, half-smiled, and almost caught each other's eye. Then they, too, went forward.

They jostled each other, and their hats bobbed forward, as if picked up and carried over an ocean by a strong east wind. I was there myself by then, in my nightgown with a canvas raincoat over it, at the far edge of the crowd, half in the grip of my fever and half in the grip of the crowd. I stood upon the knobbly roots of an oak, attempting to gain some height, but it was fruitless, and I tried to keep from keeling over. It seemed to me just then that all of us in the crowd were like a field of grass under a magnifying glass, and some point among us would catch fire at any instant, but that point kept shifting.

The car was surrounded by women and children and men, who crushed into each other for a better look. From the white and cream and ecru of the First Communicants, it was as if, with these gawkers, all colors now broke loose: lime green and buttercup yellow and red and fawn and navy blue; jostling, competing, and engrossed. They pointed into the windows and stared, and clapped their hands to their mouths, and waited, hoping for more. Men scoured the road for spent shells. Old Mr Picard, who ran the fruit shop, was on his knees in the street. His hands scrabbled about the dusty pavement for moment then they were raised aloft, clutching a shell. One man had hold of a table fork, and with it, was digging out a bullet embedded in a tree trunk by the side of the road; his smile widened with every gash he took from the bark. Another man had drawn out a pen-knife, and grabbed hold of Lloyd's earlobe, "like he was hungry for it," the *Gazette* reported later. He was about to make his first cut, when he got pushed away by a red-faced woman in sprigged calico, who wanted a better view.

Afterwards my mother sighed and said she never understood what gets into people on these occasions, it was a kind of mania, but I saw her, far on my left that day, looking towards the car, one hand shading her eyes, push her face towards it, straining, and stare. I expect we all had the same look in our eye, a look of intent, almost glassy with expectation, heedless of all else but getting more of the sight, gobbling it up, devouring it, and making it our own. The gunsmoke still hung in the air, and when I parted my lips, it fell bitter on my tongue. The sunlight descended diffuse and grainy. We all looked towards the stalled car, its motor running and its back window so riddled with bullet-holes and shatter-marks that it was as if a patch of a starry night had fallen down and crashed upon the daylit earth.

I saw Christo go forward, his soft belly wobbling. He was quickly pushed to one side. "He looked at them, all rushing ahead of him, and stuck out his chin like a left-behind child," Claude wrote in his diaries. Christo sunk down on his knees, right there in the middle of the road, and looked up at the car, which was on top of a slight incline. Some said this genuflection was act of sacrilege, no more pardonable for being unconscious; but Christo claimed afterwards it was only to ensure he had the best seat in the house. "I guess a man never knows what he's hungering after," Claude wrote, "until it's set out in front of him like a picnic."

For years afterwards, Octave Dubru maintained that he himself had sought a perfect view of the car solely in order to secure an accurate historical record. He recalled that one of the policeman had been operating a 16 mm camera, slowly circling the car, and avoiding the crush of on-lookers with the last-minute panache and controlled grace of a dancer in a crowded ballroom scene in a Hollywood movie. The 16 mm film ensured that a vision of the car and its occupants was preserved forever, and from all angles, and given that, Octave said it was a spit in the eye of posterity not to see it in the flesh if you happened to be there. Octave pressed his way through the crowd, his wide thin shoulders sticking out like the arms of an empty coat hanger, and keeping his fellows at bay. He peered through the side window. He saw Lloyd, crumpled up, with his mouth hanging open, already looking like a thing preserved in a jar, floating up against the surface of the glass.

Lloyd was in his stocking feet, Octave remarked afterwards, and that was the detail that stuck with him the most, because it made Lloyd seem so helpless. "It was like seeing someone naked," he told Claude, "only more so, because he had never seen himself like this, I mean dead, and I went away, humbled and aghast. I didn't have the stomach to look at the girl at all."

It was a matter of fact that afterwards people were far more willing to talk about seeing Lloyd in the car, and not Cammie. "If I had pushed my way to the front, I would have drawn her dress down over her knees, and not looked once the entire time," the baker told Claude Barbier, his quivering chin held steady with the firmness of his conviction. The statement was taken as one of the utmost gallantry. Only when people spoke to each other in relative secrecy, whispering in the darkness behind a porch screen in the evening, or in the gray light of early dawn delivering newspapers and collecting milk bottles, did details ever emerge. And so, talking of Cammie was a kind of confession, in which disclosure carried its own absolution.

One bullet had struck Cammie's left jaw, and passed through her front teeth, shattered them, and exited through her lips. It looked like somebody'd socked her in the mouth from the inside out, Gerard Gillian, the head clerk at the post office, said. Someone else said Cammie clutched a half-eaten ham sandwich in her hands, but others insisted she was holding a cigarette that never got lit, and at least one maintained the cigarette was smouldering and catching her dress alight but no matter, she was dead anyway by then. This one also said he had noticed a little stream of blood, a pearly, unreal pink, running from underneath her elbow. Then he realized it was her bottle of nail polish, blasted by a bullet

One night that October, my brother Henri was talking in the back hall with his friends Jimmy Pindar and Ollie Faureau, and my mother sent me to get an empty jam jar to arrange a bunch of asters in. They'd been roller skating, those three, until the darkness fell, and Henri stood there, under the yellow hall light, leaning against the hat rack, idly running one of his skates back and forth against the floor. It made a raspy sound, almost merry, rolling along and going nowhere, and so did their voices, as the boys stood there, talking into each other, their shadows merging.. *She weren't*, they were saying, *besides you know what I saw in a book, that there body part is the last to burn up in the event of conflagration like the seeds inside of a prickle-pear when you throw it in a fire.* I walked in and they went silent, and when I asked who was 'she,' and what part of you was it that didn't burn. Henri said, you ain't heard a thing, com'on, let's go by the Michard house once more but this time we'll whistle loud as we can. He started whistling, and the sound was thin and brave, and wavering. I knew the mystery they'd raised only to suppress was located somewhere within my own body too, and it was thrilling and sick-making. The sense of it swept over me like a cold wind in August. I remembered from Father Ducie that the mystery of the body and blood was to be celebrated and never violated; and amidst the jelly jars and the sacks of potatoes and the door banging shut behind my brother and his friends, I felt a wash of sorrow for Cammie, and Lloyd, too, on that very account

On the afternoon before they were to be slaughtered, Cammie and Lloyd had been seen about the streets of Saint-Baptiste, and it seemed clear from the beginning that Cammie had nothing more in mind than a visit her mother, after so many months on the road robbing banks, and bungling heists. According to the papers, their incompetence as thieves had finally caused them to kill a policeman in some lost prairie town or another, one frost-tinged dawn in February. When Lloyd attempted to blast open a safe open with the gunfire from his rigged Remington .20, the policeman was hit in the head by a ricochet bullet. At the news, opinion in Saint-Baptiste was split as to whether their ineptitude carried innocence in its copious folds like a scent of lavender; or meant merely that they were intellectually depraved, as well as morally.

Théramène Camus thought that such reckoning missed the point entirely, and that at heart theirs was not a story of guilt or innocence at all, but one of animal attraction and blood and money that predated Christian morality and would perhaps succeed it. He said as much one dinnertime while he was waiting for his brother to finish with the gravy and pass it his way. His father looked up from his dinner plate, and told Théramène that a philosopher-king was one thing, but a philosopher-dentist was something else entirely, and to hush up, he was upsetting his mother, besides which the roast was going cold. At the accounts of the death of the policeman, there were many in Saint-Baptiste who simply chose to disbelieve the papers in the first place

In any case, Cammie and Lloyd appeared to feel reasonably safe in Saint-Baptiste, and only in retrospect could one fault their presumption. On one hand, no state authority could lie in wait indefinitely for Cammie Roux to return to her hometown and walk its streets by broad daylight; for, even if those authorities had somehow surmised the project, they could hardly have predicted the timing. And, on the other, it was inconceivable that the local police, with a deputy who bestowed himself upon the local streets as beneficently as the star tenor in an amateur operetta, would summarily and without warning turn their fire upon outlaws who had blood ties to the town.

From what emerged afterwards, it was clear Cammie managed her visit as discreetly as she could, seeking not to flaunt her presence in the police officers's eyes, but knowing, if she called no attention to herself, she could count on the people of the town to say nothing. She wore her hat low upon her brow as a courtesy in this direction, someone who saw her early that morning claimed, and I imagine she had to stop herself from nodding at the passing deputy in friendly greeting

Late in the afternoon on the day before she was going to die, she was sighted at Bouchard's dry goods shop. There was a cold whoosh of air as she stepped in the door, Léon Bouchard said, and it set his skin on the back of his neck tingling. He knew without looking at her who it was. He greeted her with a nod, and not by name, and that seemed to suit her.

She stood in the center of the floor, a ray of late afternoon May sunlight slanting down upon her, "'like a drawbridge to heaven,'" Léon was quoted in the paper the next day, with dust motes spinning in its wake. Cammie looked up at the cards of trimming ribbons, set like books upon high shelves, arranged, as if by subject, by predominant color. She gazed upwards at the section of pinks and purples, which were kept in a shadowy high far corner, and Léon pulled over a footstool and helpfully ticked off the names for her: rose, cinnamon, heather, salmon, and mauve. Then she turned to consider the greens: sage, sea-grass, olive, emerald, and celadon

Jeanne-Patrice, when she read of the encounter, confirmed that Cammie had once announced to the entire history class that "celadon" was the most beautiful word she had ever heard. Cammie was importuned into looking up what it meant after sharp questioning from Sister Fanshawn, who prodded her on the shoulder with a blackboard pointer, and directed her to step up to the Webster International Collegiate dictionary at the front of the classroom. A few hours after the outlaws had been shot to death outside the church of the Sacred Heart, Léon Bouchard was interviewed by the Saint-Baptiste *Gazette*; and according to him, when Cammie looked up at the trimmings and repeated the word "celadon" after him, she made it sound like the kind of place that you read about it in a book, and hoped never to have its existence in any way sullied with actuality.

My mother said Léon was talking nonsense, and only a melancholic dry goods man who dealt day after day with bolts of fabric could hope to fashion such wistful bits of poetry out of the name of a color. "My guess is Cammie had a new dress, or more like an old one, that needed making good," my mother said. "I imagine she was wondering which green was the closest shade, and she was only thinking aloud." In any case, Cammie asked for a yard and a half of the satin-finish celadon ribbon, paid for it in exact change, and slipped back out onto the main street. Noiselessly as a shadow, a Ford the color of desert sands glided from around the corner, and stopped at the curb a few feet beyond Léon's shop. Cammie opened the car door, Léon said, and the car drove off, at low speed, in the opposite direction of the town center.

Claude Barbier was the *Gazette* reporter who interviewed Léon Bouchard. Over the years, Claude had developed a way of imposing himself on his interviewees with a kind of confidence that was in fact, only counterfeit, and dissolved at the least sign of resistance. He was broad-shouldered and barrel-bellied, but the effect they would otherwise have given, of a man of substance, was undercut by the slight stammer that overtook him in moments of conflict. He had never been outside of Saint-Baptiste for longer than a week, but he affected big city mannerisms to the extent of wearing wide lapels, and smoking so heavily that his hands had gone yellow in a single winter. His tawny, fox-colored hair had already begun to show white that year, and my mother said he held his head in such a way that you gathered the greying of his temples had given him an increasing, if baseless, sense of his own distinction. Claude asked Léon if Cammie Roux looked any different from before. Léon stood in the middle of his storeroom and thought about it. "I would say she looked wistful, confronted as she was with what she'd left forever behind."

Others, however, were less convinced. Noree Rameau ran the laundry across from Léon's shop, and she had seen Cammie as she stepped out onto the sidewalk. "What a look she had on her face," Noree said. "She was already bored, had sized up the whole of the street in one glance, and her eyes narrowed with something like contempt, mean as a starved cat's. When that car turned up, she looked relieved. No doubt about it, that girl had changed." Claude scribbled all this down, Noree told my mother, and all the while, his cigarette was burning straight down to its nub in his right hand. Claude ignored his own singed flesh in order to record Noree's quote in full. And whenever she told the tale, Noree beamed with satisfaction at the evident importance of her words.

Claude Barbier apparently liked the ring of that particular question, for he went on, a few days later, to ask Cammie's mother if Cammie looked any different after she met up with Lloyd. Mrs. Roux went on knitting. "Fifty-odd bullet holes do make a difference, son," she said. The needles clicked together again like a pair of old bones, Claude Barbier wrote down in his notebook. When he looked up, he realized his interview was over, for Mrs. Roux had quitted the porch chair, stepped inside her front door, and shut it behind her.

In his notebook, Claude had further likened the sound of the knitting needles to the bones of a hanged man rattling in the winds of history. I saw the annotation myself, years later, for Claude Barbier donated his collected papers to the Saint-Baptiste Public Library. They were wrapped inside a manila cardboard folder, bound up with butcher's twine, and stored in the humid and gloomy basement: uncited, moldering, and half-crumbling. The building, with its battered doors, sagging shelves and blackened floors, looked as though it had survived fires and floods, earthquakes and wars, and various other Acts of God. In reality, the only Act of God this deserted building, in a forgotten town, ever suffered was time, a calamity that was gradual, but in the end no less devastating.

While Cammie was in the dry goods shop that afternoon, Lloyd was by the backwater, a few hundred yards from the Church of the Sacred Heart. Father Ducie was out clipping the hedges in the relative cool of the afternoon, because earlier that day, Philippe Beaufils had proved disappointingly haphazard at the task. "He was hardly any better as an altar boy," Father Ducie admitted to me with a sigh, three decades later, "but his father did sponsor the church's annual Italian night." As he was clipping the line of hedge that looked out over the street, Father Ducie saw a beige Ford parked under the sweeping green branches of an oak. When he completed one side of the hedge, he turned the corner, and faced out over the backwater, and there he beheld Lloyd Cannon wading up to his ankles, in his dark suit with the trouser legs rolled up.

"I can still see the scene in my mind. The blackness of his figure put everything around it in sharper relief, as if the trees and the water and the grass and so on were all converging upon him," Father Ducie told me. He raised his right forefinger, and his gray-green eyes were magnified behind his high-prescription spectacles. He regarded me like a reproachful and studious old lizard. "Lloyd Cannon was like the hole in a doughnut, the emptiness by which the substance is defined," he concluded. He lowered his hand, grasped his glass of iced tea on either side, and gave it a small oracular swirl. He had lately been reading the Jesuit theologians.

It was rumored from the first that Father Ducie may have known more than he was telling of the matter, for Iphigénie swore she had talked to Cammie the day before she died, by the water fountain in front of the library. Cammie, she claimed, had not only promised to see the First Communion, but also confided her desire to have

Father Ducie hear her confession. Iphigénie had been standing in the library's front hall, squinting up at the message board, hoping to find a notice for a pair of used roller skates, when she'd seen Cammie hurrying past the open door. Judging by the time of day, and the direction she was going in, Cammie was probably on her way to the fabric shop. Iphigénie ran out to her, and held onto her hand, and kept her standing there in the sunlight.

"I was telling her about my First Communion, and the dress my mother had made for me, trimmed in pinks like she knew suited me. Cammie said oh she'd love to see it, and to remember our illustrious leader Napoleon always said the greatest day of his life was the day he received his First Communion. But still she did look sad, then she said how she longed to "unburden her soul to the Lord, and seek the absolution of saints.""

Iphigénie whispered all this to her sister Andromaque, an hour after the bodies of the outlaws had been laid out in the backroom of Monterose's furniture store and tinctured for display: Claude Barbier, waiting in the crowded shop room corner for an interview with Dr. Camus, who was performing the autopsy, overheard, and took notes. "Absolution of saints" was not the kind of words anyone would have imagined Cammie using, if they'd been trying to sound like her; nor, for that matter, were they much more likely from Iphigénie.

Drawing a parallel, my mother pointed out that the formal and specialized nature of the diction Bernadette of Lourdes attributed to Our Lady did suggest the girl had indeed seen a vision. On balance, my mother was inclined to believe Iphigénie - regretfully, though, because Iphigénie had an unfortunate habit of staring at adults, including my mother, when they greeted her, and grasping the hem of her school uniform into a small ball high above her knees, then running off, like a wild thing set free, down the main street, or into the woods. "Revelation is a gift," my mother said that night, firmly, and in a way that made it clear she was doubtful of some of the choices the Lord had made in bestowing it. She was mending one of father's shirts, to calm herself down after the afternoon's bloodshed. She was so deep in thought and heedless of the gaze of others that she bite off the thread with her teeth.

Eugenie LaFarge, Perpetuée's oldest sister, backed Iphigénie up on this subject, but only in part. "I saw Cammie in church, out of the corner of my eye," she told Claude Barbier on the afternoon of the day on which the outlaws had been slaughtered. "She was standing in the left-hand entrance, the one Father Ducie enters the altar from. It was near the beginning of the ceremony, and she hovered there a moment, a blur of light like a fleeing angel. Then she was gone. She hadn't come to see the First Communion though, because as soon as she saw what was underway, she disappeared."

Most people agreed that whatever Iphigénie may have told her, Cammie, even if she did enter the church, wouldn't have expected to find Father Ducie, on a Wednesday, performing a First Communion. When I asked him, thirty-four years later, whether he'd agreed to hear Cammie Roux's confession that day, Father Ducie turned his head to the side, and one eye looked me unblinking and unselfconscious, like the eye of a day-old trout resting on a bed of ice. He gave me a nod so brief I wondered if I had imagined it. "What did she confess to?" I asked. The question fairly escaped from me, when I exhaled. Father Ducie paused. He leaned back, and his chair creaked. "You know I am not permitted to answer that question," he said, "and I know you were not raised to ask it."

What is certain is that when Iphigénie insisted Cammie stop and talk outside the public Library, someone else saw her too, and in retrospect, Claude Barbier pinpointed this as the crucial moment of her, and Lloyd's, undoing. "Let's not be melodramatic," my mother said, when she read the *Gazette*'s account the next morning. "She was bound to be spotted sooner or later the longer she stayed in town. You have to wonder if she half had it mind herself." My father poured himself another cup of coffee, and said that the notion of a death wish is as melodramatic as they come. My mother nodded, because she was not really listening, and turned back to the paper. Jeanne-Patrice sighed and looked at her sorrowful reflection in the kitchen window, and Henri availed himself to the last of the coffeecake. The air was already warm, and gathering. It bore down on us with the weight of a dead thing. Somewhere outside, a door slammed and a dog barked, and for no good reason whatever, I burst into tears.

*   *   *

The afternoon on the day before the outlaws were to be slaughtered, Sherriff Charpantier left the police station around twelve-thirty. It was his regular lunchtime, and, almost without exception in the years he had been in Saint-Baptiste, he took the meal at his desk, eating companionably enough, but sharing nothing. On this day, however, he headed out of doors, and made his way to the library. He was returning a picture book for his son, which was already two weeks overdue. As the major law enforcement officer in town, he hoped, it seemed, to spare himself the indignity of being sent a late notice. He was walking up the hilly, magnolia-lined path to the library's back entrance; slowly, I imagine, for I had never seen him proceed at any other pace.

Christo Badarde, on his way to the hardware shop for a new garden rake (his mother had announced the night before that growing sweet Vidalia onions were her one consolation in this life), passed him and nodded hello. He wondered briefly what would bring Charpantier out in the middle of the day by a building inscribed with the words *Plaire et Instuire;* but when he glanced at the book, as big and square as a phonograph album cover, and as colorful as a jar of jelly beans, the reason seemed clear enough.

Charpantier was not the kind of man you joked to, however, least of all about himself; and while several people had seen him carrying the children's book that day, not a single one made any comment. In the mind of the town, it was that lack of jocularity over the boy's picture book, more than anything else, which came to stand as evidence of Charpantier's hardness, and fundamental status as an outsider. "It was the dog that did not bark in the night," Balthezar told my parents one summer night on their porch. He was grim-faced, and white-lipped.

As Charpantier ascended the curved slope that led to the library door on the day before he was going to kill them, he must have glimpsed Cammie through the flowering branches; ascertained her, bit by bit. She would have come into his focus piecemeal, then all at once swum into totality: her hair, the line of her face, the sound of her laugh; perhaps, if the wind were right, the trail of her flowery dime store scent, until finally, he had no doubt of who it was he was looking down upon.

He did not enter the library: *Billy Braggart's Biggest Birthday* was not returned until five days later, when the son himself, with a quivering chin, and a nickel moist with his sweat of his palm, proffered payment to Maria Bernard, the town librarian. Maria smiled disapprovingly and a little absently, for she had been swapping details with colleagues about the dress Cammie had been wearing when she had been slaughtered, and if she'd really smoked cigars, like they'd said. Maria dropped the coin into a drawer without looking, and rejoined the conversation.

On that afternoon before the First Communion, Charpantier returned to his office, book still in hand and shielding his heart. He made two phone calls, one to Baton Rouge, and another to Dallas, Texas. He did not say much of anything to the two part-time officers who were in the station at the time, anything at least that they could, or cared to, recall. At this time, Balthezar was still patrolling the streets of the town with a half-smile on his face and a gentle lilt to his walk, drifting peaceably through the fallen petals of the cherry tree blossoms. Having come to his own understanding with the outlaws earlier that day, through his appointed emissary Louis Sante, he had no idea that "the forces of unsubtlety" as he was later to term them, were marshaling to supersede his own considered design.

I was sent to bed that night with a slight fever, and despite my constant ministrations to my new white shoes with a bottle of polish, my mother informed me I would not be able to receive my First Communion with my classmates. The next morning I woke early, slipped noiselessly and with resolve into the dress I had longed to wear (Alice in wonderland blue, with a smocked yoke), and a pair of canvas shoes. I cast myself into that gray dawn like a diver into deep and uncertain waters.

As the years went by, it was not clear to me precisely what I could have had in mind in mind, traversing the deserted streets of the town that morning, in a First Communion dress and my oldest pair of shoes. I expect I wanted to see the church bedecked with flowers, and satisfy myself of the day's preparations, though I never made it that far. In my mind's eye, I can still see four cars arriving over the hill into town. They are steely-gray, and make a line of shimmering metal with nothing trailing after it, like a needle without a thread, poised there a moment and about to puncture the dawn, and the fabric of the town forever. But that image is no doubt an instance of hindsight, an accretion of dreams and memory and conjecture that implicates one detail then another, amplifying some and discarding others.

When I was passing through the woods that lay to the east of the side of the Church of the Sacred Heart, I came across some men I had never seen before, cutting down lumber, or digging a ditch, I thought, although I did not ask. Then I saw a pile of guns leaned up against a tree trunk like the framework of a tepee, and a man emerged from behind it and smiled with crooked front teeth, and said, not to worry there, little lady, we're just having ourselves a turkey shoot. It was the wrong season for a turkey shoot, and I made to hurry by, but another of the men stopped me, stood in my path, and told me I better get on home, I had no business being out there, especially without my momma.

"Town's not safe for decent citizens," the man by the gun-tree said, and somewhere to my left, a third one, who I did not see but only heard, added, "Yet," and spit. They all laughed, a rough-edged gravelly laugh. The morning mist was heavy and bluish, and it curled all around their figures. They were like a trio of ghosts, laboring towards no good end, and I was glad to leave them behind. As I walked on, I looked back, and the white of their shirts shrunk behind the curtain of green trees until it was the size of a pinprick.

I crossed through the town center, and cut through the park behind the town library. Beside a sloping bank of azalea, Lloyd Cannon was standing, upright and dark, like a figure cut from black pinstripe and pasted in. I was brought up short, but he grinned easily and without irony. Close-up, his eyes were the mildest blue I had ever seen in a grown person. He smelled of cinnamon spice and soap, and he had an azalea blossom in his right hand.

"These here are Cammie's favorites," he confided, in a stage-whisper, as I approached. "For her to remember Saint-Baptiste by." He winked, and went on, "You won't tell a living soul who made off with them, now will you?."

He snapped off another flower, palest pink though I would have guessed Cammie favored the crimson. I had no business being there myself. I nodded but said not a word to him about what I had seen, and nothing to anyone else either. I headed home, entered the house through the back door we kept unlocked in those years, and crept back to my bed. All through the morning on which the town's outlaws were blasted to bits outside the Church of the Sacred Heart, I was mostly asleep.

In the annals of the case, Balthezar's "dog that did not bark in the night" was not the only dog involved, for Charpantier had devised his own homespun stratagem to ensure the outlaws drew to a halt. Towards that end, Charpantier enlisted the one creature he surmised Lloyd could not refuse, or rather, refuse to Cammie: the big old yellow hound her momma kept tied up to the side of the house. In the last hours of the night before the outlaws were to be shot to death, Charpantier personally staked out Mrs. Roux's chicken coop, cajoling the dog and coercing him out from under the house, where he slept, with a sliver of ham. Under a soft black sky, by the light of a crescent moon, Charpantier slipped a length of rope around the hound's neck, and led him away. The dog was so old he hobbled about on three legs, but Charpantier appeared not to have figured this into his plan, which was this: the agents of law would lie in wait by the side of the backroad which led from town to Mrs. Roux's farm, and at the approach of the outlaws's car, the dog would be released into the road, and Cammie would no doubt demand Lloyd stop.

In the event, the dog was too old and lame to rush into the road on command. Two state officers called in from Baton Rouge attempted to shove him from behind, and one from Dallas ran across the road, with bent-knees to keep from being seen, and called him from the other side. But the dog lay down in the sun-dappled pine-needled shadows and yawned, his eyelids drooping as if it were coming up to the hottest day of the year. He roused just as the police rifles were taking aim. He heaved himself up on his three legs, and began to howl. But by then the gunfire was exploding all around him, and it drowned out his alarmed yelps.

In the aftermath to the shooting of the outlaws,

Théramène Camus took a particular interest in this matter, which, as an ironic counterpoint to Balthezar, he called "the dog that did not jump into the road," and considered as the comic chaser to an essentially tragic event. He came to feel the ruse was fundamentally misconceived, and summed up a sentimentality about dogs and children and for that matter, prostitutes, that the public and police erroneously ascribed to the criminal element. As a supplement to his amateur interest in journals of history, and his professional one in dental bulletins, he had turned to reading detective magazines. He deplored their sensationalism, he said, but admired their scientific spirit.

In Théramène's opinion, Charpantier was, like many policemen, too blunt an instrument to ever probe the human heart with any degree of acuity, and it was when he most strove to show insight that his emotional myopia was most in evidence. Théramène was willing to bet Lloyd would have simply driven around the hound if he had run out, or even hit him, if it came to it, and kept on going, and Cammie would have understood. This was not a story about a girl's love for her dog, after all, he said once, with a knowing snort, at his father's dinner table: did that dog even have a name, he challenged us as he passed along a bowl of roasted potatoes. "Bunglers," he muttered, shaking his head, as Dr. Camus asked him for the second time to pass the bowl of green beans upstream. Iphigénie, who had invited me there, and was enjoying a spell of popularity because her father had performed the autopsy on the outlaws, was finally compelled to reach across her brother's plate for it herself. And in my heart, I was glad, because for once I had heard the charge of ineptitude directed not at Cammie and Lloyd, but at their antagonists.

As he was pouring the gravy over his roast potatoes, Dr. Camus remarked he never could understand why Lloyd had developed such a fixation with wading in the backwater, which everybody knew was shallow and brackish and afforded no good view whatsoever. Mrs.

Camus looked up from her plate and moved her head from side to side as though she was stretching the muscles in her neck after years of maintaining the same posture. It was often the case, she said, that the hero in Racine's tragedies lived in a walled palace that looked out over the sea, and whether black or grey or deepest azure, the sea stood for vastness and escape and nothingness all it once. It was the first time I remember ever hearing her speak a full sentence, and I looked at her, astonished.

So I was not in the church the day that the outlaws were riddled with bullets. I ought to have been there, receiving my First Communion, my hair pulled back with pale-pink ribbon, and my smocked dress the color of cornflower. My bedroom smelled of shoe polish, for up to the last moment I was certain I would be there in church, and the last thing the night before, had buffed white my Sunday shoes in secret. But my fever got worse instead of better, and at the hour which the town was to recall with vivid if conflicting clarity, I was back in bed, sipping orange juice through a straw, while the radio in my mother's kitchen played *The Romance of Doctor Annabel Kent*: the woman doctor who longed to be both a doctor, and a woman. In my sickbed, I lay back, closed my eyes and pictured myself in a white coat, stethoscope and high black pumps, enjoying a similarly tortuous, stiletto-punctuated walk through endless and immaculate hospital corridors.

Later, I would swear that the story line that day featured Annabel Kent's decision to treat two dying outlaws, regardless of their crimes, and the Texas ranger who had expressed two incompatible vows: first, to see the criminals were shot dead, and second, to marry Dr. Annabel Kent. But my mother was certain that the events of the day had entered my fevered brain, and colored my memories after the fact. *Annabel Kent* never broadcast on a Wednesday, my mother said; and she remembered that, as she'd stood at the oven and stirred a pot of chicken broth, she'd been listening to the news, and arguing with the disgraced chief of the department of weights and measures, who'd been indicted for soliciting kickbacks. Folks don't take pride in their work the way they used to, she concluded. When she told me that, I thought she was wrong: the outlaws did, and so did the folks who hid in the hedge, and blasted them to smithereens. Already I was asking myself if Louis Sante wasn't proud of what he did, or didn't do, and Father Ducie too, and everyone in town, in fact. I wasn't the only one asking that, either. For within the hour of their death, the outlaws cast a shadow that proved our town was a thing of substance, and had a story to tell. The blood that bound us together as a community was theirs.

For sure, they had shed more blood than their own in the course of their career. But when they'd killed anybody, it was never around here. It was to the west, or to the north; in states with endless fields of wheat, or grasslands shaggy with a coat of reddish weeds, or slicked over with a hard glaze of frost. In Saint-Baptiste, it was widely intimated that Cammie and Lloyd only ever killed armed police, and only then in self-defense. We knew that was not entirely true, but thinking that it was let us carry their tune, which came to us in unexpected moments, and keep it all in key. Now and then, a newspaper tried to tell us of the lives the outlaws had wrecked, and how our thoughts and prayers ought to be sent towards those victims. And they were, but soon they all drifted back to Cammie and Lloyd, like a snowfall blown back by a strong wind. In memorializing their victims, we could not help but memorialize the deed, and in time, the ones who had done it.

For example, to evade the police outside Albilene, Lloyd had need of a car, and he spied one, with the keys in the ignition, parked in back of a hash house. He had trouble starting the engine, however, and the owner ran out from the diner, and attempted to wrest the wheel from Lloyd's thieving hands. He wound up shot through the head, this man, who had a wife and four children. His oldest boy had just won a scholarship to study chemistry at the state university; but he had to give it up, and support his mother. He wound up taking a job repairing farm machinery. Never leave a vehicle's keys in the ignition, my father warned, the incident serving as a extreme reminder of the need for basic prudence.

It was soon said around town that the man who'd owned the car had dealt in stolen goods himself, contraband cigarettes and heirloom jewelry; or else was a bank officer, who for years had made a career foreclosing on folks in trouble without so much as a fare-thee-well. Details of this kind were tried out on porches and in front of shops and at the counter of LaFarge's. But a silence brooded afterwards, like an on-coming headache, because such excuses were no good, and we knew it. They were futile and false, and we cast about for some words that would frame the event so we could look it straight-on as best we could, square our shoulders, and go about out business. Thésée supplied them.

"It was like a movie," Thésée said.

He was stocking the candy display at the gas shed at the time, and he paused, with a handful of fireballs. He gestured to evoke the wide arc of light emanating from a projector to the screen, and the gesture betokened not dismissal or remove, but the greatest respect. Whatever distance Thésée put between himself and the effects of such an event on those involved was borne not of apathy, but of reverence.

Thésée went on and said how somebody ought to make a movie about them, and the movie should be a western, with the two of them in a car that trailed through endless fields of golden wheat; and the wheat parted, but once, to allow their progress, then rejoined; the sky unfolding, blue, unanswering and vast, above them. He held his hands out flat high above his head to demonstrate to sky part. His little brother Mithridate, who was stationed in front of the cigarettes, and was armed with a water pistol, said no, it should be a gangster movie, with cars and guns and wise guy cracks that came quick and easy as the gunfire. Henri said it was slapstick from beginning to end, a pair of fool crooks haring around, and the police as inept as the crooks. Jeanne-Marie said, no, it should be a musical. She seemed possessed by the spirit of Cammie Roux herself when she said it, for she was breathless with her own conviction, and heedless of our reaction. She put down the can of tomatoes she'd had hold of, and raised her chin to meet their laughter.

And standing beside her, I could picture it. Each member of town would be going about the business of their day: washing windows, baking a cake, delivering a letter; and each would stop a moment, and sing a lyric; and thus the story of Cammie and Lloyd would be told, with borrowed breath, and communal effort. It was as Théramène would say: they were our blood relations, each and every one of us, for by shedding blood, of others and then themselves, they had defined us as a town.

The blood that the outlaws shed was not incidental to our town's fascination with them. It was crucial to it, and never more so than after their deaths, for it was as though a refrain for their ballad had at last taken form. We knew they were criminals, and I never heard anyone suggest otherwise; but as Théramène said, focusing on the rights and wrongs in that way was something priests and schoolteachers and newspaper editors insisted on doing, and it just didn't get to the heart of the thing, or in any case, the whole heart of it, which he as an historian was determined to do. "It's a mere story to you," Dr. Camus told to him over Sunday dinner some weeks after the outlaws had been slaughtered and laid out for all to see. (By then in the waning weeks of her popularity, Iphigénie had invited me over. I accepted at once, as she promised we could sneak into her father's study, and handle the implements her father had used to dissect the pair).

That day, Dr. Camus was wearing a shirt the soft green of a wintergreen cream. All his shirts were in an array of muted shades that, by comparison, made Lloyd Cannon's look like a string of cartoons, or something pulled out of a magician's hat. Sandalwood scent faintly rose from him, and lingered in his wake. His watch was gold, and it hung on a little chain that dangled from his vest; and though I tried not to think it, I began to feel my own father was sorely lacking.

"You've never had to witness a mother hearing the news, how she shrivels to the ground in front of you," Dr. Camus went on. But, Théramène pointed out, in case of Cammie's mother, that we had; and moreover, there was nothing mere about a story. "We killed them, and we made them immortal," Théramène said, and he picked up his fork and started in. It was a phrase Théramène was often to repeat in the coming years, for, he said, it struck him as neat and complete as a reflexive verb, or a gunshot and its report. Théramène put the phrase forth in the conversation more than once, and I picture it balanced there like an Easter egg on the bowl of spoon: closed, and perfect, and symbolic of some deeper mystery.

This was an incident, Théramène went on, that cut right into the flesh and blood of the town. He maintained further that everyone in town had partaken of the outlaws's crimes by so much as talking about where they'd been the day the outlaws were shot. "A mother gives us life, and a father gives us a name, but no less than these, are the outlaws our blood relations," he declared. A pea fell from his fork.

Dr. Camus looked at his oldest son, and said he figured that's what he'd been longing to hear all his life, a dentist with a cosmology. Iphigénie was eating up the last of her dinner, and her knife clinked against the plate. Her mother turned her head slowly, for she was surely weary with the effort of holding it up so high. She looked out the window into the mid-distance at what appeared to be nothing, and, in her light toneless voice, told Iph not to bolt her food so.

In later years, Théramène tried to recreate the earlier, modest, success he had with the article on the founding of Saint-Baptiste, by researching the life and demise of Miss Cammie Roux. But the article never materialized. I doubt he even penned the first word. "I lived through the events," Théramène said twenty-nine years after the outlaws's blood had run in the street, "and perhaps that proximity has stymied me. Some chroniclers gain by nearness to their subject, but for sure, I am no John, or Mark or Matthew."

"How about Luke?" his seven-year old daughter said. "Weren't he a doctor, too? A real one though, not just for patching teeth." She was lying on her stomach on the parlor floor, a girl near-sighted already, her nose an inch away from her coloring book as she scribbled in it. Théramène frowned, gave the box of crayons a peevish little kick, and told her carnation pink was no fit color for a lion.

Théramène was not the only citizen of the town to have ghost memoir that hovered over him, with a beating of wings so far on high that he was no longer sure that he heard them. There was another chronicle that never came to pass, though it was many times foretold, as Balthezar alluded to it for years without seeing the need to write it: *A Lawman Speaks*. It did not exist outside his premature reminiscences about the writing and reception of it, which were dispersed in a random and self-important fashion. Before he had even bought the paper on which to write his memoir, Balthezar was already anticipating reviews of the work, and drafting responses to them. On occasion, the phrases of those rebuttals leaked into his everyday speech. At a high school graduation years later, for instance, he was a speaker, and early on in his address, he lost his place, fell silent a moment, and recouped by announcing, "A lawman is not a means of production." He raised his right hand straight into the air as if he were taking an oath.

He was clearly alluding to Pope Leo XIII's encyclical riposte to Marx, *Rerum Novarum*, my mother said; but the reference was lost on the bulk of his audience, who were fanning themselves against the heavy,, humid air with the front page of the graduation program. The seepage of Balthezar's thoughts meant he was not washing in a full tank, my father said. Balthezar was never promoted, not even after Charpantier's heart failed the week before Thanksgiving, six years after the outlaws were gunned down outside the Church of the Sacred Heart. Charpantier was at a poultry farm up by Lynn's Ferry. He had nabbed a turkey, and was holding it by its neck, the bird squawking all the while. According to a newspaper account, Charpantier fell down heavily, stage by stage. At the first tumble, when Charpantier was on his knees, the turkey fought loose, squabbling, until all Charpantier had in his grasp was one of its legs; and at the second stage, when he had sunk down to his stomach, the turkey had sprung free altogether. It rose off the dun-colored ground for a few feet, gliding over a black-iced puddle. It hit the ground again, with ridiculous skedaddling feet, and fled further from the corpse of its would-be executioner.

But Balthezar always looked as though he should have been sheriff, my mother said. As she poured more cream into her coffee, she sighed.

*   *   *

It was as if the fate of the town, and its desire, were from beginning to end to be a witness. Being a bystander was a positive ambition, and Cammie and Lloyd had obliged, providing the occasion, at some sacrifice to themselves. In time, people veered from putting themselves at the center of the event, or at least on its whispering outskirts, and having a story to tell, to knowing nothing of it, and being in the clear of the reach of gunfire and the spattering of blood. Some made the circuit there and back several times.

Christo Badarde, for example, was to add to his embellished recounting of Lloyd's gospel of everyday living, the claim that the morning the outlaws were shot, he had seen Cammie waiting in the shadow of the Church of the Sacred Heart. She shrunk against the wall as I passed, he said, but the whiteness of her gloves gave her away; and he told her that if she came by a little later, the church would be open, and there would be a First Communion for her remember Saint-Baptiste and all its children by. When it then got said that Christo had led the girl to her death, and that news got back to Christo, his chin shook and his belly wobbled like a soft-set egg, and his frank and vulnerable eyes filled with tears. "It wasn't the day they was shot that I saw her by the church," he would say, begging you to listen. "It must have been the year before. Yes, now I remember." And he wiped his eyes on his shirt sleeves, and sniffled.

Henriette Grenier, the seamstress, was at first taken with the thought that she had seen the first inkling of the ambush, but then the weight of the responsibility undid her. That winter, on a night when the air was glacial and windless, she contracted a fever. Three mornings later, she woke up to find her hair had turned completely white, and that day, the wind came up again, with a rush of might as though it had been resting up, and brought down the stoutest branch from the live oak outside Monterose's.

The death of the outlaws was not just an incident in time. It occupied space as well, for the stretch of road where Cammie and Lloyd were shot to bits became a landmark as fixed in everyone's minds as the post office or the baseball field. The smell of gas from the punctured tank of the Ford lingered in the hot couple of days that followed, until a warm nighttime shower washed it away. The splotches of blood on the roadway faded to the color of brick; and when another rain came, there were only rusty-looking shadows left. Finally, about a week after the death of the outlaws, Henriette's sister Odile, who did the housekeeping for Father Ducie, could stand it no more. She crossed the road around noon, armed with a bucket and a floor brush. She scrubbed ferociously at the splotches till they were no more substantial than the dazzlespots in your eyes when you look too directly at the sun.

For a while after the shootings, people in cars or on foot drew to a stop by the stretch of road. Sometimes they seemed to have come expressly for that purpose. Others, on their way inside the Church of the Sacred Heart, would stand on the top step, and turn, and look across the road, to give impression their interest was only incidental, as they bowed their head and blessed themselves. Mrs. Dubru left a bunch of blue irises by the side of the road. Someone else followed with a bouquet of lilacs, then a spray of larkspur, and finally a bunch of mixed wild flowers. Taking lemonade on my mother's porch, Father Ducie said he hoped this most recent offering would be the last, as it was the most appropriate to the couple: for, before they had gone wrong, they were as lilies of the field, who toiled not, and not even Solomon in all his glory was arrayed like one of these. And Balthezar bowed his head as though deep in thought, and inhaling the statement's truth, and said that certainly was the case.

The floral offerings ceased, but they were in time succeeded by another commemoration. Twenty-one years after the outlaws were slaughtered, a community college sprung up over in Acadia. It was built of yellow brick, and festooned with brightly colored banners. The school offered courses in dental hygiene, accounting, secretarial sciences, and the dramatic arts. Its first year of operation, the drama students were bitten by a bug for relevance and social realism, and conceived the idea of re-enacting the slaughter of the outlaws. "If this is their attempt to follow the exhortation, 'épater le bourgeois,' they can think again," Théramène was quoted in the *Gazette*, when he was asked to comment on behalf of the World Historical Society. But Théramène no doubt underestimated the force such a spectacle of re-enactment can have.

The college put an ad in the papers appealing for the use of an old Ford, and finally, secured one from a beet farmer over in LaFayette parish. The car was yellow, and though not the color of desert sands, was deemed close enough. The director of the drama department, a young man with liquid brown eyes and the pitted skin of a lizard, appeared at the St Anthony's Guild Easter fete. He wore a pair of black levis, and affected a mumble. "He looked like a thug from the chorus of a stage musical," Théramène said. The director bypassed the baked goods table without a second glance, and went directly to the rack of used clothing. Father Ducie approached him, ascertained the nature of his business, and frowned. Then, thinking the better of it, he began rummaging through the rack himself, and proffered some items he felt might be of particular interest. "All the proceeds do go to charity," he reminded Mrs. Carmina, who was in charge of the baked goods table, and had been watching the goings-on with simmering outrage. Perhaps sensing his interest may have gone too far and given a wrong impression, Father Ducie did not attend the event himself. He stationed himself at the front window of the rectory, by the green plaster figure of Our Lady, and watched. The curtain fluttered every so often, my mother said, so she knew he was there, watching.

Most people in Saint-Baptiste deplored the enactment, some because they felt any restaging of the death of the outlaws was inappropriate; and others because they resented it was outsiders that were doing it. I was far away when the first the re-enactment was staged, but my mother wrote and told me about it. Her disgruntlement made itself felt in such detail that I could only conclude she had been there herself, watching from an enviably situated vantage point.

Despite their official irritation, most residents of Saint-Baptiste did attend, hoping perhaps if they paid close enough attention they would be in a position to spell out all of the play-act's many failings. The college set up stalls selling doughnuts and coffee along the stretch of road where, long ago, Lloyd had pulled over in his Ford to help Christo Badarde fix a tire, and tell him about life. To anyone who knew the town, it was a haunted landscape. But the grease in the air, the mid-afternoon sun, the smell of stage make-up and coffee grounds, and the pre-arranged clamor, no doubt drove away any ghosts that might have been tempted to linger.

As Father Ducie declined to have the church involved in the event, the spectacle was limited to the roadway where the ambush took place. It rapidly took on the feel of a grade-school pageant. Charpantier was played by a fellow who stuffed a pillow under his belt for the belly. For the rifle fire, they enlisted an arsenal of cap guns. The programme's high point was supposed to be the final look that passed between Cammie and Lloyd just before the shots rang out. But the stage-master, who was hidden in shrubbery, reached up to shoo away a bluenose that had been buzzing by his ear, and he inadvertently rustled a branch of cherry laurel, which had been the signal for the gunfire to commence.

When the shots rang out, the stage Cammie was still looking out the car window, and had yet to turn her face towards the stage Lloyd. At the sound, Mrs. Favereau, her skin by then as mottled brown as a mushroom, burst in tears, and her son had to lead her away, though he kept looking back towards the drama the whole time, my mother reported. And the wiry-haired spotted terrier Théramène's wife was holding in her arms broke into a fit of yipping, and did not quiet down until she offered him a morsel of chocolate from her pocketbook. Even then the creature was on alert, nervous and inconsolable the rest of the day.

At the miscued shooting, a frown passed over the actors's faces like a shadow. They simply ignored the first volley of shots, and completed the look in their own time, with gunfire and small bursts of smoke already exploding all around them. By the time they were ready to go into their death throes, the guns had run out of caps, and so the pair had to convulse and contort to some rhythm completely of their own making. Then they slumped and went quiet, and waited, uncertainly, for applause. None was forthcoming. After a moment or two, the director stepped forward from the clump of chickweed where he'd stationed himself.

"They're right," he told his actors, loudly enough for everyone to hear, "It would be like applauding the Our Father." At that, the two actors rose, their Cammie stumbling a bit in her unaccustomed heels, and their Lloyd not making a bit of effort to help. The crowd parted to let them pass, except Perpetuée LaFarge who stood her ground, glared, and made them walk around her. For a while, no one said a word.

"Cammie read detective magazines, not true romance, and Lloyd never would have worn a white shirt with a beige tie, and in actual fact, the car approached from the south side, where cape jasmine used to be," Théramène told my mother, by way of greeting. He had watched the event sullenly, his behind parked on a log, with a sandwich in a brown paper bag beside him. My mother thought he was out of joint because the drama school had not sought him out as an expert in local history.

As it turned out, the troupe had no interest in ascertaining what any of the actual participants may have said or done. "I see it more as a silent movie," the director explained to Joseph Nidier of the *Gazette*. His hands floated through the air as though imitating the swaying of sea grass in a current. They were sitting in LaFarge's superette, the day before the staging. Théramène happened to be there too, a few tables over, my mother reported, and at the director's words, he sat up, as if despite himself, he sensed a kindred spirit, and was not sure whether to be threatened or pleased.

It occurred to me, as I read my mother's letter, that what was most striking about the staging were not the features it had, but the ones it did not. Its lack of verified speech only set the tone for its more fundamental and significant lacks: the Church of the Sacred Heart, the First Communicants dressed in white, and, finally, the outlaws, the Eucharist, and bloodshed itself. There was no real presence, and in what was only a reconstruction, there could be no transformation.

News of the re-enactment sat ill with me. It was as though a sun had gone out in our Catholic sky; and I could picture my mother hovering in a corner of it, urging me to beware the chill vale of Protestants. But I had already confronted that prospect the moment I first faced it, on the morning when the outlaws were slaughtered outside the Church of the Sacred Heart and the First Communion was disrupted. The police called "Halt," and dissembled, as the priest stood at the altar and proclaimed: "This is my body, and this the cup of my blood." In that moment, words were torn asunder from things, and the order of things itself was recast, and diminished. It was the despondency of doubt that made a religious out of me; and not fear of life, but a glut of it, that sent me on a career of contemplation. There was no love I could bear, or faith I could uphold, that could hope to outdistance or overpower the sight of those shattered bodies on the road. In time, I became a bride of Christ; like Cammie only in this: I wore a ring for a groom I had abandoned, but could never escape.

Balthezar attended the re-enactment. My mother told me he positioned himself in the sunlight a good hour before the event began; and stood there like a sentry of posterity, at attention, with his shoulders thrown back, and his brow implacable. When the drama director stepped forward, signaling the event was over, Balthezar nearly clicked his heels in response. He departed in the manner of a foreign dignitary at a state funeral, giving a short nod of recognition to a select few in the crowd, and maintaining correct posture throughout. "Now, that is a gentleman," my mother wrote.

"Perhaps it was inevitable that the killings would transpire first as tragedy, and next as farce," Théramène wrote in a letter to the *Gazette*'s editor a few days later. "I never thought I would find myself quoting the doctor of all *philosophe* Karl Marx with evident approval and fellow-feeling, but that is just what the spectacle last week has compelled me to do, when wars and strikes and economic depressions could not." My mother sent me the clipping of the letter, and she had penned a comment along its margins: "and you should see his neckties these days."

The staging became a more or less annual event. The players and directors changed, but that hardly interested us, for it was the audience we were watching. Dr. Camus, who had stood on a cane on the outskirts of the proceeding the first year, suffered a stroke by the time of the seventh; and Josephina Rabideau died in her sleep after the tenth. The children of the First Communicants began to appear in the crowd, teetering, over the years, on the edge of adulthood themselves. To them, it was already merely historical, and they smiled at the wrong places, and drifted off to the doughnut stall at the time the stage shots were due to ring out.

And nine or ten years into it, Lloyd's baby sister, by then a gray-haired old lady, bug-eyed and sad, turned up. The first we ever knew of her existence were the old lady shoes as they emerged from the door of a powder-blue Chevy, and steadied themselves, first one and then the other, onto the compacted dirt. She was clutching an oversized pocketbook full of inch-square patches of the coat Lloyd died in. "$100 a patch," she announced, in a flat Texas voice, and with a pugnacious set to her jaw, as if somebody was arguing with her. A few students from the community college stepped forward to examine her wares. We of the town stiffened our necks and looked away, because knew our bond to the event was stronger than any scrap of fabric, however stained in blood it might have been; because we had been there, and Lloyd was ours.

IV

The event defined the town not just in the eyes of its own dwellers. In those few days that followed the slaughter of the outlaws, the gaze of outsiders was upon us, and forever after, their view impinged upon our own, and redoubled it.

Reporters from all the surrounding states, and as far away as New York and Chicago, swarmed into Saint-Baptiste by that afternoon. A number of them set up shop up at Dubru's rooming house, and a few of them slept on the floor of Josephina Rabideau's dance studio. For a few days, the reporters crowded into the drugstore and the barbershop, and took over the café. Roland's accustomed place was occupied one night by a stringer from Joplin, who in preference to engaging in conversation, hummed stray bits of show tunes; and the next, by one from Dallas, with a sleepy smile and the eyes of viper, who some said afterwards weren't but a gawker who carried a note book for cover.

By six that evening, LaFarge's ran short of bread and ham. The next morning, LaFarge rose early, and was compelled to barbecue a pig before its appointed season. Smoke filled the air, heavy with grease and spiked with salt.

Old Mrs. Favereau thought the events of the previous day were being replayed, and she ran, screaming, into the road to prevent the carnage.

One of the reporters was from Boston. He had glasses with thick round lenses that turned to blank discs when the sun hit them right; and a massive head of black curls that was disproportionate to his shoulders, which were as narrow and neat as a shirt just turned out of its box. He regarded everything that came his way with an inquisitive self-confidence that was more studied than it was steadfast, for he had as well a quick nervous way of snapping his head around as if perpetually on point of being hailed by some person unknown. His accent was a nasal honk, and, to me, as fascinating in its myriad contortions as a hitherto unimagined birth defect. When I encountered him around town, I tried not to stare, but my eyes were unfailingly drawn back to the source of such noise.

In line for a cup of coffee at the superette, the reporter stood aside and, with a bow, let the locals go ahead of him: he was overheard telling Claude Barbier, with a rueful smile and a slight shrug, that he felt himself taking on the manners of the town as easily as its accent. Claude inhaled the aroma from the cups of coffee set in front of them as if he was at last breathing in the air of a big city, and he smiled back in wordless and grateful communion. The Boston reporter announced that he was determined to find the one particular aspect of the story, "the still point in a turning world" as he told Claude, from which the truth of the matter would be seized. A shard of sunlight had caught the Boston reporter's spectacles at that moment, and a bit of steam from the coffee fogged them up further, and rendered them blank glass surfaces which reflected, and took in, nothing. At this point, perhaps to save face, the reporter took up his coffee cup and announced to Claude that, as far as he was concerned, there was no doubt that the matter of greatest significance was whether the police had called "Halt" before they opened fire.

Though Claude Barbier did not take a single note while with the reporter from Boston, and hardly seemed to blink in response to the man's conclusion, Claude's story that afternoon was headlined: "The 'Halt!' Not Heard Around the World." Among the civic-minded, the crying or not crying halt became the moral hook from which to hang their impressions of the event. A pair of bandits breaking the law was one thing; but the law breaking the law was something else, a trick of perspective, that was still novel to us, and it made us catch our breath. And so, that question became for awhile the focus of interest, regret and speculation.

It figured, for instance, in Father Ducie's sermon the following Sunday. In it, he prayed for all those not given a chance in the last instance to save themselves, and he contrasted human justice, imperfect and unmerciful, with divine. Balthezar was sitting in the third pew, and he raised his head at the words as if he was accepting an honor, for they did surely affirm his own intended design. Charpantier, sitting far in the back of the church as a late arrival, gave no reaction whatsoever, and only continued to pick at his teeth, and grin through the entire service, as if he were partially deaf, and re-living some private joke. Three of the five lawmen who had fired the fatal shots were still in town, but as they were from Texas, and there was not a Catholic among them, they did not hear Father Ducie's veiled reference to their handiwork, though one gathered they would not have much cared if they had.

"I was sorry to bust a cap on a woman," Henderson Parker said, "especially one that was sitting down." Henderson Parker was the chief ranger, called in from Dallas. His complexion matched his calfskin jacket: rough-hewn but fine-pored; and they looked to have both weathered a thousand days of rain. He wore the jacket even with that warm spring sun beating down upon him, and he refused, steadfastly, to sweat.

On his last day in Saint-Baptiste, the Sunday following the event, Henderson Parker stood on the train platform, and gave a final interview to the *Saint-Baptiste Gazette*. He was lean in the way that speech is taciturn, or a building is spare; and his very frame seemed faintly contemptuous of another's excess. When I first saw him, I wondered what his belly must have made of Charpantier's; but I had to accept that in the end, they'd got along well enough to achieve the business at hand.

Henderson Parker refused to speak to Claude Barbier, on account of his having raised the crying halt issue in the first place; and the honor instead went to the stringer Joseph Nidier. It proved to be the pinnacle of Nidier's reporting career, a premature peak, the heights of which he could never scale again. In time, interview came to seem to him a curse by which his own past rose up and mocked him. Later in life, he would sit in a dark corner of the café, looking to snare passers-by and tell any one of them who would listen of the time he'd interviewed the man who shot dead Cammie Roux. In such moments, Nidier's mouth wobbled, and his hands shook, and he looked intently into the listeners's face as though they did not believe him; and indeed, as the years went by, there were many who did not.

"I never liked the look of the fellow," my father said as he sat at the kitchen table, reading the *Gazette* the Sunday morning Henderson Parker left town. He said it as though he had spent a lifetime studying Henderson Parker's features, and drawn his conclusions cautiously, over time. "I doubt he ever did call 'halt,' " my father went on, "or rather, I suspect that he did, but he did not mean anything by it."

Henderson Parker's "Halt!" was not a command, for it carried no import towards the ones ostensibly addressed. It existed only to cover the reputation and the public conscience of the one crying it out. It was intended for Parker's benefit, and our own, and not for Cammie and

Lloyd's. Privately, after much discussion, my mother and father had come to this determination: Henderson Parker did cry halt, but that the word was shattered by bullets and blasted to bits at the very moment the lawman gave breath to it - just before their bullets turned, and rained down upon the two outlaws. Henderson Parker said the word, barely; and in the view of my parents, and myself, it was a declaration of faith that was first riddled with bullets, on the road outside the Church of the Sacred Heart at the moment the Host was consecrated.

That was the way I heard my father put it: "faith," not "public trust," "honor," "justice," or even "fair play." The dark undercurrent of my parents's reasoning, as I came to understand it, and made my own, was the unspoken but ever-present realization that the "Halt" would have been falsely intoned as the priest stood at the altar, raised the host, and said the words, "*Hoc est enim corpus meum*": This is my body. I pictured the scene more clearly than if I had actually witnessed it, for in my vision it was purified of all accident. The host was raised on high, half talisman, and half target. The "Halt!" was launched, like an arrow tipped with fire, from Henderson Parker's lips, and it sped, so swift it had no need of stealth, towards its mark, and found the heart of the sacrament, and stopped its coming to pass. Instead of the body and blood of the Lord, we were left with the body and blood of the outlaws.

But from the beginning, Théramène thought the whole question of whether Henderson Parker cried halt or not was misguided - "hopelessly misguided," he would amplify, as his hairline receded and his sense of his own importance hit high tide. He has inherited his father's pomposity but not his gravitas, my mother said; and Théramène eventually become, in order, the town's only dentist, its first resident to secure a private telephone line, and later a television, and the founding patron of the Saint-Baptiste World Historical Society, with a fat golden ring that gleamed from his pinky finger. The longer he ran with the herd, the more he was determined to be the maverick. Cammie and Lloyd, he maintained to the end, as he had from the beginning, were not a story of guilt, or of the law, or of moral rights or wrongs; but of carnage, and carnality.

Thirteen years after the slaughter of the outlaws, I was still seeking my way in the world, and avoiding for a time the road my heart had laid out for me. I embarked first on becoming a schoolteacher, and for a little while longer, reported for the *Saint-Baptiste Gazette*. In both pursuits, I spent my days asking questions to which I more or less already knew the answer. Affirmation was too easily attained, and made me despondent. That mania for questions will turn your heart to stone, my mother warned me. She was taking a peach crumble out of the oven as she spoke, and she had to avert her face from the blast of hot air.

She need not have worried; for all the while, I was turning over in my mind another precept that my mother had imprinted upon me: "A cake is done when it pulls away from the pan." To me, my mother's precepts of domestic life carried a lower-case oracularism about them, and I stowed that particular entry away waiting for the time it might at last apply to me, whatever the consequences. I pulled away at last from the surroundings that had formed me, and I left Saint-Baptiste.

Fourteen years after the event, then, to confirm the route I had elected upon, I went on retreat. It was a term I always liked because it implied that, previous to it, I had been engaged in a momentous battle from which respite was required, and I was in the company of generals and archangels. I arrived by train to a parish in the west of the state, far removed from the blue-green sea, the smell of crawfish, and the groves of myrtle and althea. I headed instead into a part of the world where the only things you are certain to meet up with are grass and cattle and distance. When the train approached my destination, late in the afternoon, I watched the red dust rolling up in little clouds along the tracks. I thought of Charpantier, for it was the kind of earth I always imagined he had sprung from, and into which the Lord had breathed His spirit.

I can still remember how I encountered Louis. It was within a few minutes of disembarking. I was carrying my mother's black valise, as square and compact as a closed prayer missal. The moment I stepped down from the train, the case was sealed with a coat of fine red dust. I was wearing a black skirt, unfashionably long, and it threatened to sweep the ground as I passed over.

Adjoining the train station was a small gas shed. It stood on a raised platform, like a lighthouse that had lost its way. Louis was standing by the cash register, counting coins in front of an open cash drawer. I saw him first through the window, framed there, surrounded by boxes of cigarettes and chewing gum and shoelaces. I recognized his face right away, almond-shaped and sorrowful. Through the years, it seemed to have only grown into its mildness, succumbed to it from within, as if melting to the touch of some slow-burning, interior flame. Though his hair had faded, and seemed touched with gray in certain lights, he was one of those who never particularly age because they had never been particularly young.

When I entered the station, Louis looked up, and I greeted him by name. He looked blank, and I pressed ahead, feeling somehow reckless and that I was showing my hand, and told him my own. He was neither awkward, nor surprised. He remarked on the heat; then, indicating a small, rickety picnic table set out in the center of the floor, he invited me to sit down. He opened a bottle of lemonade, sat down himself, and asked me how my folks had been. His manners had never failed him. I willed my own to rise to his level; for the question I found hard not to ask - it fairly danced on the tip of tongue like a curl of fire and singed the roof of my mouth - was what Louis had done, and not done, on that day so long ago, when the outlaws, one of them his fugitive bride, were blasted to bits outside the Church of the Sacred Heart.

About everything else, he was candid, and well-considered. He listened judiciously, and declined to nod, in either agreement or denial. He paused to let his thoughts come forth in his mind, and took the time to find the words that did them justice. He had come out here the same way I did, taking the train to the end of the line, or what had been the end of the line those fourteen years before. I gathered he had been intent not so much on making a beginning as on ascertaining there had been an end. He never spoke Charpantier's name, letting me instead sully my tongue with it. Louis gave no reaction to hearing of his death, and I was never sure if he had heard of it before anyway. He only sat back, expressionless, and watched an oil truck rumble by outside, into the fading sunset. He remembered Cammie's dress on the night they had been married, and he even smiled a bit at the thought of the flowers she'd left in the bathtub. He spoke of his father, with a distance that was matter-of-fact but not cold.

"A father can't choose his son, no more than a son can choose his father," he said at one point, or "allowed," more like, for he seemed throughout our conversation to be granting the world a series of dispensations he had been accumulating over time. Things would have been different for Gabrielle if her momma had lived, he went on, and that went for his daddy, and himself too. He looked at his empty glass, and shook his head. It seemed dangerously like the preamble to his getting up from the table, and I had no choice then but to ask the question.

"You think that pair needed any setting up?" he replied.

He looked me dead in the eye, and I looked back, unblinking, like a gambler who's just rolled the dice, and watched them turn up a calamitous sum, final and incontrovertible. "Or needed me to watch them die?" He stared glumly at his hands. And in that moment it came to me, that while the outlaws's need for an audience was likely, the town's need to be one was incontestable. I asked him why he'd taken a gun that morning, and was surprised only that he did not deny it.

"I was on the look-out for my daddy," he said. "Expect I wanted to prove myself to him at last, so as he'd not forget it. But I never did have a gift for killing." He paused and his face curdled suddenly into a small smile. "And not much of one for living neither."

When I'd started down this path of questions, I had been careful to leave a last sip of lemonade in the bottom of my glass, so I would have something to pick up, and drink casually, to draw out our conversation. I made to take up the glass at this point and direct myself to unraveling his ambiguous answer. I was on the point of asking him what he wanted with his daddy if he'd found him, and how he meant to prove himself that day.

The light was going cold and flat, and his eyes were square upon me. They almost dared me with their defeat, and shamed my curiosity with their weariness. I fell silent. He held my gaze, and the way the light hit his eyes made them look nearly colorless, like plugs of nickel. When I next spoke, I was asking why he'd gone and disappeared. And the feeling rushed over me that the whole time I'd been interrogating a ghost, one who'd got caught in the last of the day's light, and could not escape it if he dared dissemble.

Louis leaned back in his chair, and the legs scrapped against the floor. With that sound, it was as if his disclosures had somehow been breached. He paused a moment before he spoke. "Ain't like you got the okay to hear confessions, now is it, Sister?" He grinned, but his eyes were without warmth. He looked out at the sky, which was blazing up cold and luminous just before it went to dark. "She found her own way to death. I loved her, and we had been married once." Then he set his indifferent gaze upon me. They were unyielding, his eyes, and offered no quarter. "Remember that, even if you can't understand it."

I felt like I had been slapped; but in response, I held my head high, and well back upon my neck, as though it already hung heavy with a veil, black not white, and not of airy lace, but of good stout serge.

V

In the end, the bodies of Cammie and Lloyd were carried from Lloyd's bullet-ridden Ford to the furniture shop on a couple of full-sized baker's peels. There turned out to be no other way. When the police had pushed the crowd back and held it at bay, Charpantier ordered Lloyd's car towed, with the slaughtered outlaws inside. He reached into the car himself, on Lloyd's side, and turned the motor off. When his fat face emerged, it looked as though he'd been holding his breath. One of his men, Lollo Duane, brought forth a chain, and used it to attach the police car to Lloyd's V8. He got into the police car, and fired the engine, and dragged the Ford the color of desert sands out of the small dip in the road. He hauled it forward a few hundred yards. Silently, we turned and watched the Ford car move forward with its dead occupants, and under another's power. Lloyd was hunched over the wheel as if he was still driving, except when you looked closer, and saw that the top of his head had been blasted away to a bloody pulp. Then the police car sputtered, groaned, and drew to a stop.

Charpantier barked out an order to get that damn thing moving, right now. But as soon he looked into the crowd, saw its stirrings and sensed its low ominous murmur, he knew it could not wait that long. Lollo Duane tried starting the car again and again, but it shuddered and choked and finally sent a puff of steam into the air, before the engine went dead. Charpantier stood facing us, as if he had suddenly found himself on the wrong side in a stand-off. The metal of his gun glinted at his belt, and the smoke from the spent shot was still settling hazily over the hedge of sweet mock-orange. The splotches of blood out on the road were already thickening. A host of flies arrived, buzzing in lazy circles over Lloyd's car. Then the door on Cammie's side swung open. Her arm fell downwards, and her painted fingertips dangled an inch or so above the road.

Charpantier kept his gaze upon the crowd, as though willing us to stay put with the force of that alone. After a few moments, Poirier the baker stepped forward. His apron was stained blue with frosting. He held out his hands in a gesture of entreaty, but he was, in fact, offering up his implements for police use. He kept two broad pallets, he said, which he used to hoist the largest batches of bread into the oven. He described what he had in mind, with a sequence of efficient gestures, and Charpantier assented with a short nod. Poirier returned quickly, "in a twinkle of a sheriff's badge," as my father said. He laid the pallets on the road, beside the running board, and never turning his back upon the car, he walked backwards and rejoined us, the watching crowd.

There was trouble turning the bodies onto the pallets, because, at first, the two officers assigned to the task seemed unwilling to touch them, let alone hoist them aloft. They began by merely tugging at the arms, then almost immediately dropped hold as if their fingers had been burnt. They did not look at each other, but stood there a moment, facing into opposite horizons, and wiping the sweat from their brow. Finally, taking a deep breath, they pitched their back into the task, and hoisted Lloyd onto a pallet.

His mouth was already gaping open, and with the movement, his head was jostled to one side, and his jaw fell open wider. It looked as if a scream had escaped from those parted lips, absconded straightaway from the realm of sound into silence, like a thing eternally being still-born. As they swung Lloyd's body aloft, his coat flapped out, and a coin fell from the pocket. It landed flat upon the road. Octave Dubru rushed forward, and before anyone could stop him, snapped up the coin. Nineteen years later, when he was on his way to Moreauville to buy some bedding supplies, his car slipped on a puddle of spilt oil, and collided head-on with a produce truck. He was buried with Lloyd's quarter stowed safely in his suit coat pocket, for he had thought ahead, and left instructions. A man from the *Gazette* turned up at his funeral to report on the story, and took a photo.

Then the officers turned to Cammie. You could tell it she weighed less, for their backs barely bent at the task, but troubled them more, for when it was done, one of the officers went over to the side of the road and retched into the tall grass. The other officer waited respectfully, his head bowed. The crowd too kept still and silent. It wasn't a matter of sympathy. We were too busy breathing, and taking in the sight. "What I will always remember is the smell of her hair," the officer said later, "like she'd just washed it in chamomile tea, and her face all riddled with shot."

Charpantier directed his men to carry the pallets into town, two men each. They lifted the pallets onto their shoulders, and raised the bodies on high. By then, Balthezar had emerged onto the scene, and taken in what had happened. He gave Charpantier a look of unpardoning reproach, then looked to the heavens, and blessed himself. He took his place at the front of the procession. The four brims of pallet bearers's hats swiveled towards each other in inquiry. Their shoulders gave a shrug. It was Balthezar who led them forth into the town. We followed, casting the shadow of the living over the dead. I was at a distance from my mother and father. I saw them through the jostling elbows and shuffling knees of our neighbors, but it did not occur to me to run and join them, because we in the town were united in purpose: to bear witness, and take a gander.

Out in front, one of the officers from Texas, his eyes as lackluster as spent shells, took his revolver out of the holster, and kept us at bay from the bodies of the outlaws. Charpantier trailed along, his belly wobbling and a smile breaking out on his face now and then like the sun on the first warm day in March. Lollo Duane was further behind, stationed in semi-disgrace to watch over Lloyd's car. I turned back to look at him. He was peering into the driver-side window, shaking his head in disbelief, almost smiling. Then he lifted his hat as if in salute to the vehicle, or its absent driver, and he turned and slouched, stoop-necked, his weight against the driver door.

The only funeral home in Saint-Baptiste was the back of Monterose's Furniture Store, and we all knew without having to ask where the procession was headed. It did not take long get there, and throughout, Balthezar kept his head up high and his shoulders straight as an example to us all, but especially to the pallbearers. When the shop swung into view in front of us, Lazar Monterose was already waiting on the front step, clutching a broom as though readying an establishment for houseguests.

To make room for the two bodies of the outlaws, and allow them to progress into the backroom, they had to push aside a heavy, three-piece mahogany bedroom-set Lazar Monterose had just put on display. It took three men to move, the papers reported later, and the bed's clawed iron feet left deep track-marks on the floor that lasted long after the bloodstains in the road had been washed away. The crowd piled in, as many as could, but the shop was small, and the rest of us waited outside, impatient and implacable in equal measure. Then, with Charpantier on one side, and Father Ducie on the other, Dr. Camus stepped forward from the crowd.

He was scented with a hint of bergamot. His shirt was magnolia broadcloth, and from his hand there trailed a handkerchief of silky pearl-gray. The crowd parted to let him, his aroma, and the many fine cloths upon his person to pass through. Perpetuée LaFarge took the opportunity to sidle in next to him and sneak by, until a hand reached out from the crowd, grabbed the side of her veil, and yanked her back amongst us. She did not bother to howl. We regrouped slightly, and waited.

Charpantier appeared briefly on the threshold of the shop. His broad forehead glowed in the heat, and he hitched his face into a smile, which fell down around his chin in short order. His hat was in his hands, and he gave it a half-twirl. "Folks," he said, "you'll get your chance to look when the state gets through cleaning up after itself."

At some point that day, a whisper rippled through the crowd that Lloyd's daddy had arrived from wherever it was he came, to view his son's remains. If I sit still enough and let my memories collect, I believe I saw a white-haired man, unfamiliar to me, who hovered at the far edges of the crowd. His shirtfront was as blinding as a splotch of sunlight; or so it seemed to me, though the fever may have bubbled into my eyes just then. He picked his way, his head bobbling a bit, and circled towards the back of Monterose's. When next I looked, he was nowhere in sight.

It seems that after the old man had seen what he'd come for, they'd set him up on a rocking chair, on the small back stoop of the shop, which is where I saw him next. He was raised on high, and alone. The sun was hot and the air was still. The old man took out a broad white handkerchief. By turns, he fanned himself with it, and wiped his face; and then, overcome, he wept into it.

One or two people stepped around the side to look at

him, and they murmured a report on his doings, but soon, everyone lost interest in him, and sometime that afternoon, he slipped away unnoticed. It was not so much a measure of compassion on our part, this inattention, but a recognition of the truth: he was not part of what had happened. His son, by contrast, was one of us forever. Once more, without the distraction of interlopers, our eyes were trained upon the shop front.

My brother Henri had been swept inside Monterose's with the first wave of onlookers. "There was a stack of coffins leaned up against that lattice-wood barrier in back," he told us, "behind which Cammie and Lloyd were getting worked on. One of the Beaufils boys climbed up on the caskets to get a look. He slipped and fell and Mr Monterose screamed at him to stay put, but by then too many other people were clambering all over the stacked goods, too." In the end, Lazar Monterose was reduced to standing in the middle of the shop floor, swatting easy targets when they came his way, and chewing his gums in between. Folks were pressed right up into other, and against the lattice barrier, waiting, and breathing up used air. Balthezar stood sentry to the backroom entrance, Henri said, like an angel in sepia, and he never looked inside the backroom once.

According to Joseph Nidier, a young woman in the crowd managed to press in so close to the back barrier that she actually breathed into the face of Fénelon Favereau, who had been impressed into assisting Dr. Camus. Panicked by such proximity, Fénelon took up a bottle nearest to hand, and began squirting embalming fluid into the crowd; whereupon the townspeople retreated as though before a spectacle of holiness. Then Fénelon drew back, and fainted. His spine slid down the length of the wall until his tailbone hit the floor with a bump, and he did not come to. Dr. Camus called upon Father Ducie to replace Favereau as a witness; and upon Théramène, to take notes of the proceedings.

The autopsy was characterized by happenstance from beginning to end. As recorded by Théramène, the report was incomplete, misspelled, and in places, simply incoherent, salt-and-peppered with the odd Latin term that appeared from the blue without reference to the requirements of syntax. Dr. Camus was to take the report as further evidence of Théramène's middling abilities. Théramène also wrote it in pencil, and his script become less distinct as the report went on, and the lead went blunt. No one had noted the choice of implement at the time, but it eventually put the legal standing of the autopsy under question, until Dr. Camus was compelled to pen a postscript that vouched for the findings and their authenticity. When he was first called into the back room of Monterose's, Dr. Camus said he would need his instruments, and Charpantier dispatched Thésée to retrieve them. But the boy came back with an incomplete set, and to perform the autopsy, Dr. Camus had recourse to some of Lazar Monterose's carpentry tools. He requested a butcher's apron, too.

"Lloyd Cannon," Théramène's first page of notes began. "An inch-long tattoo above the right elbow, of an angel, titled 'Grace.' Cubitum." A scald mark seven inches long and an inch across at its widest ran along the left flank, a disfigurement, we found out later, from when Lloyd had upset a pan of boiling water over himself as a toddler, when his youngest brother was getting born. One bullet had shattered the eighth vertebrae, and another grazed the twelfth and fractured it in two. In his right hand, Lloyd had been holding an old wooden-handled pistol, which was struck by a bullet and disabled; shielded by the useless firearm, that hand was un-maimed, but the first three fingers on the other one were shot completely off. The left eye had received a direct hit, and exploded into a mass of pulp. One bullet entered just below the right nostril, and exited through the base of the skull. The forehead had been pelted with shattered glass from the windshield, and Dr. Camus took a pair of pliers and extracted several shards, which were put on display in the foyer of the town library, until displaced seven months later by some first editions of a regional poet based in Port-Royale.

On the torso, Dr. Camus noted twelve bullet marks on the left side, and twenty-seven on the right. Théramène asked himself in the margins of the report, "Why? Position in car?" Then Dr. Camus prodded the flesh over the liver with a putty knife, and remarked that it at least seemed intact. He made only a single, deep incision, over the left upper torso. He peeled the skin back, up towards the neck, took up a small wood saw, and began carving through bone and cartilage. The dust flew up in tiny particles, dry and hot amidst a surrounding spray of moisture, like a tooth getting drilled, Théramène observed afterwards. Dr. Camus's hand sweated, and the saw slipped, but only once. Then Dr. Camus put down the instrument, and scooped his hand into the cavity. For a moment, he held in his hand the stilled heart of an outlaw. One bullet through the left ventricle, he said, and Théramène noted the finding down.

At this point, Father Ducie stepped forward from the far corner of the room, where he had been standing, quietly sweating, and saying the Rosary. He wiped his pale moist brow, and hurriedly blessed the body. The rosary was still dangling from his fingers, and it rattled as he made the sign of the cross, Théramène said later. "The gleam of the knife confused me, with that heat, and those everlasting smells," Father Ducie told my father. "I thought they would start pulling things out of him at any moment, and this was my last chance to bless him before they got hold of his innards. Also, I knew that if they ever did cut into his belly, the stink of guts and feces would floor me."

In the end, no one did cut into the belly. Satisfied with his examination, Dr. Camus concluded with what everyone knew from the beginning: the cause of death was multiple gunshot. Théramène wrote the phrase down. Each of them affixed his signature on the report. Théramène's skittered over the page, in illegible, uneven loops, for, as he told us, his hand was by then so sweaty that the pencil was slipping in his grasp.

In the month afterwards, a couple of anonymous letters were sent to the editor of the *Gazette*, lamenting the hicksville shoddiness of the autopsy, and the failure to examine the internal organs of the pair out of simple respect for professionalism. But whoever wrote them was in the minority, at least as regarded Lloyd. Anyone who had been there that day knew that Lloyd's insides, and out, were so criss-crossed with bullets that it was those bullets, and the routes they took within him, that were holding him together. "For sure, the bullets riddled him," Théramène said, "but by then he weren't nothing but riddle." In total, 51 bullet holes were tallied; though at dinner tables in years to come, over the brandy and in the company of men alone, Dr.. Camus would give a small smile, and let it be known that there were in fact many more than that.

When they turned to Cammie, Théramène took a step back, swallowed, and moved the notebook up in front of eyes. Executed as it was with no firm surface behind it, Théramène's handwriting was more wavering than before. The report reads as if they had set about delaying the actual examination of the body, for it begins with an inventory of Cammie's personal effects: two gold wedding rings, a diamond ring, and a crucifix around her neck. The items were removed and placed in the bowl of Charpantier's hat for safekeeping, because by then, Lloyd's enamel stickpin had already gone missing from where they'd laid it down on the floor.

Dr. Camus noted the subject was wearing a red dress and red shoes. "A tattoo six inches above the right knee," Théramène continued, "with two hearts and an arrow through them, the left heart labelled 'Cammie,' and the right heart, 'Louis.' One bullet wound, entering an inch to the right of tattoo and exiting through the femur." Dr. Camus counted seventeen bullet holes in the arms, legs, and shoulders; and twenty-three more in the torso.

The abdomen was slightly bloated, he noted in an aside, and Thérämène duly recorded. No doubt it was this that led to rumors that Cammie was with child when she was gunned down. Whenever he was asked about it, Dr. Camus gave a small, pained smile that forgave but registered the questioner's blighted intelligence. He always denied the possibility, and said the woman had clearly partaken of food in the hour before her death. When he was in an expansive mood, he cited the half ham sandwich that had been found in the front seat of the car and entered into the automobile's inventory. But his failure to cut into the body, and close the matter with certainty, evidently haunted him in years to come.

The *Gazette* once interviewed him, and asked if there was anything he would have done differently "in the course of his long career," and everyone in Saint-Baptiste knew what was meant. "Taking a puff on his pipe, Dr. Camus looks out the window at his marshmallow-pink camellias," the *Gazette* wrote, "which have been his pride and joy since his retirement seven months ago. 'That woman's internal organs,' Dr. Camus says finally. 'If I'd looked into them proper, we'd all been spared the prittle-prattle.' "

Thérämène said afterwards he could barely look into Cammie's face laid out on the slab before him. One bullet had entered through the right jaw, and exited through the upper lip, and in its trajectory blasted off a front tooth, almost entirely. "It is the image of that tooth I will carry with me to the end of my days," Thérämène said, shaking his head. For him, it seemed to sum up the fragility of all things mortal; and he returned to his dental texts with renewed purpose, approaching reverence. I used to see him when I went over to play with Iphigénie. He opened one of his text books, and ran his hand over the page, the way a seamstress does with a yard of silk, or a master carpenter a plank of fine mahogany: for what before him was solid and good; and the stuff, through his efforts, from which more good would come.

Overall, the report on Cammie was shorter than Lloyd's, whether because the heat and smell of embalming fluid and the mutterings of the crowd had finally gotten to Dr. Camus, or because of Théramène's personal distaste for the exercise. The blood was already coagulating on the wounds, Dr. Camus noted, and a clear sticky fluid had emerged from the corners of Cammie's lips, and on Lloyd's chest, where the cut had been made. The flies had begun to arrive in thicker clouds, and their droning was so loud and steady as to be almost palpable. The wall of live flesh watching through the holes of the latticework pressed ever closer, Théramène said later, and he felt the eyes of the town pressing down upon him like the weight of water. My brother Henri was among them.

"We were packed in there so close and sweating so much that after a while you couldn't smell anymore where you left off and somebody else began," he said that night, marveling and happy. He was in his pajamas, and his face was flushed pink because he had just gotten out of the bath. "Somebody way up ahead of me was sweating something fierce, and I watched the drops trickle down his neck, and you know what - all of a sudden I felt them, same as if they was dripping down my own back." His eyes widened as he relived the sensation. My mother was sitting, working on her mending, and her face was half in and half out of the lamplight. She stabbed the needle, deliberate and precise, into the shirt sleeve, drew the length of the thread out high and straight, and without glancing away from her handiwork, told Henri to watch his mouth, or he'd be sitting in that tub for a week. Henri went a shade pinker, like somebody had slapped him, and he clammed up for the rest of the evening.

All in all, fifty-nine bullet holes were counted on

Cammie's body. The time of death was entered as 9:45 am, the same as for Lloyd. The witnesses each signed the second report, Théramène said, and Dr. Camus stood back, took a deep breath, and stretched his shoulders. Then he called for Lazar Monterose, and the waiting crowd seized up like a face in the grip of an oncoming sneeze. We knew why he was being called in, and without saying a word or catching a single eye, Lazar headed out back to fetch a bucket of water, and a basket of clean cloths.

We stopped to watch, some of us with our mouths open, and others caught with a mouthful of cake – for under police instructions, Poirier had retrieved the cakes he made for the First Communion reception, and hoisting a tray upon each shoulder, made his way through the crowd, pausing when it was called for, so that each who chose could partake. The day was by then so warm that the confectionery tuberoses had softened, given up their shape. The coloring leaked out in miniature puddles of indigo and carmine.

Charpantier emerged from the backroom. The crowd inside the shop parted to let him through. He stood on the front step, and waited, though he did not need to, for silence. "Folks," he said, "they'll be cleaned up soon, and you'll see something you won't soon forget." By then, even he seemed weary, and his fine fat belly sunk a bit as if deflated. For, of course, the town had already seen something it was never to forget, that day that the outlaws were shot to pieces outside the Church of the Sacred Heart on the day of the First Communion.

Charpantier was looking into the horizon, as though he was searching for one last thing, of proper significance, to say on this occasion, when the Lt. Governor's car pulled up. Charpantier grinned, slowly and with satisfaction. The driver emerged, opened the door for the Lt. Governor, who lumbered out, bulky and dark in navy pinstripe. Charpantier raised a hand in greeting, for while in the larger world he was only a political minion, here on his own turf, he was in command. The Lt. Governor set his hard-surfaced sun-glassed gaze in Charpantier's direction, but did not wave back.

"Who's that man anyhow?" Perpetuée asked loudly. "He cousin or some such to Honore Dubru?"

Her father never answered, for by the time he opened his mouth, Danny Brunet had already jumped out from the back seat, and was coming around the front fender of the Lt. Governor's car. He looked bashfully up into our faces, as if he wanted to thank us for being there but was too shy to express it with anything but his eyes. Even then, I believe I was aware of how he strove to bear the weight of his fame lightly; nonetheless, his smile slipped, and went crooked, and his footwork was a little off-balance, as he picked his way through the waiting crowd towards the shopfront.

He was a few hundred yards away from Monterose's bottom step, and Honore Dubru drew back his cane to let him pass. Faced with a show of deference from the afflicted, Danny Brunet stopped, and gave a deep bow, with a broad forward sweep of his arm. As soon as he moved forward again, he was watching us for our approval, and he tripped with a heavy thump of his shoe over the exposed root of a sweet gum tree. Without a second glance to anybody, Danny Brunet cut a caper there and then. Several times in succession, he almost but not quite fell down, and you could almost hear the musical riff that would have accompanied such a routine in the movie house. Finally, he stood up straight, and made to tip his hat to us. "How bout that?" he said. All over, people's faces were easing up, and Danny Brunet looked into a field of grins, and grinned himself because he knew he was the day star that had brought them to the blossom. It seemed as if his fame, and comic timing, had broken the spell of the day forever.

Mr LaFarge stepped forward, still shaking his head and

chuckling, and asked for Danny Brunet's autograph, and so did Perpetuée, of course, crowding in front of her father, and spreading out the folds of her lamentable veil for Danny Brunet's admiration. Thésée Camus ventured forward, though he later denied it, and the reporter from Boston raised an eyebrow, and curled first one end of his lips and then the other, so the end result was a kind of smile. He moved in too, jostling with Mr. Charvet from the town clerk's office, and the ice-blue organdy hat of Josephina Rabideau, which was vying dangerously into the ken of a chocolate brown cloche swathed in dotted black net. Suddenly, Danny Brunet was at the center of a commotion that was growing in size and intensity. I could see only flashes of him. It was as if he was a card in a deck getting shuffled, as people collided into each other in their rush to get next to him. And all that flesh and intention directed his way looked likely to both salvage him, raise him up, and tear him asunder.

Then Charpantier's voice called out from the direction of the shop threshold. "Hey folks," he said, "come and get it."

And Danny Brunet was caught in the crush, the swell of people that turned, with alacrity, from crowding him so close they seemed to be almost holding him upright, to over-running him. I saw his face. He was momentarily bewildered, then he went blank. We piled in and his face was swept aside like a straw hat carried off in a high wind, first in one direction then another. In the end, he was deposited on the furthest edge of the crowd. I turned in my progress towards Monterose's, and looked at him. He was standing under the sweet gum tree that had been his undoing, and he still clutched, crumpled up in his hand, an autograph paper someone had shoved at him, and forgotten. His face loomed among the branches, and it was greenish-white, like a just-peeled apple. Disdaining to look our way, he kicked at the exposed root one more time, and cursed.

The bodies of Cammie and Lloyd were not the only artefacts to be worked over and speculated upon on that day. The Ford sedan the color of desert sands was emptied of its guns: six Browning Automatic rifles, twelve .45 Colt automatics, and three .38 caliber automatics; as well as the pistol that was pried out of from Lloyd's dead hand. There were sixteen license plates, from states as far-flung as Wisconsin and Nevada and Vermont; a china figurine of a ballerina in a purple tutu; a grocery bag full of canned peas; a half-eaten ham sandwich; a pair of sun glasses, with the left lens blown out; a road map of east Texas; a powder compact; three books of sheet music; a saxophone; and over six hundred rounds of ammunition. One officer rummaged through the car, turning his head toward the shattered window to call each item out, while another officer stationed himself in the full spring sun, and wrote them down in a pocket notebook.

Charpantier stood in the shade of his hat, and watched. When the task was done, he assigned the car a guard. Lollo Duane, charged with the duty, grew quickly bored, and tired. Within the hour, he had leaned himself against one side of the car, staring steadfastly off into the distance where it was shady. This lapse allowed a gaggle of boys to sneak along the other side of the car, by the hedges, and peek in. They claimed also to have nabbed a few items they found stashed under the front seat: a detective magazine bannered "Circus Terror Preyed on Tots!!", a page of sheet music for "It's Hard to be Bad When You're A Good Girl (and Nine Miles out of Town)," a handful of bullet casings, and a half-used tube of lipstick, in Eastern Rose.

By early evening, the car was hooked to the back of a police van brought in from Port-Royale. I watched Charpantier as it went past him. He was standing by himself, at the side of the road in front of the drugstore. The dark was already falling, and bluish shadows thickened over him. Like a respectful onlooker at a funeral procession, he turned his face to follow the car's passage out of town; and indeed, with that car, his own moment of glory was passing before his eyes, around the corner, beyond what his gaze could claim.

Within a month, we learned, the car had been stripped down to its chassis. The front fender was auctioned at the Port-Royale celebrations for the feast of Saint Blaise, and fell into the waiting hands of a fresh-faced and suggestible Civil War buff, who gave in to an inchoate desire for artefacts of bloodshed from the present day. The back fender was commandeered as a trophy, first by the head councilman in Baton Rouge, who stashed it briefly in his office on top of a file of old property assessments; and then, upon hearing the election results that fall, shipped it on to Lt. Governor's mansion, where it was reworked into a fire surround in the second floor ballroom. The seats were shredded by bullet shot and stained with blood that had dried to rust. They did a few circuits with a traveling sideshow, and wound up in a gamblers's haunt in the north of the state. They were put on view by the coat rack at the exit, behind a velvet cordon; a parting sight, the manager said, sure to chasten the winners, and comfort the losers. As for what remained of the car, there was dispute. Some insisted it provided the chassis for the car used in the community college enactment, but Théramène said that was romantic nonsense promulgated by those who would forever confuse historical reconstructions with history as it really happened. "Those are the kind of people who give amateurs a bad name," Théramène told my father one day in the post office: he was mailing in his subscription to *Historians Today*.

Others were certain that the authorities destroyed what remained of the Ford car the color of desert sands, breaking it down and scattering the parts to deprive the legend a focal point of chrome and paint; or that the police made off with the pieces themselves as relics and souvenirs; or that they found that the car was stolen, and returned what remained to its rightful owner; by one account, a tobacco shop owner up in St Albans near the Canadian border, who dealt in bootleg, by another, a ginger-haired divorcee in deepest Kansas. Over the years, reports would emerge from places all across the United States that the death car of Cammie and Lloyd had been definitively located and identified, but we in the town felt superior to the whole business, which by then was dirty with the ink of newsprint. We did not need the body of Cammie and Lloyd's car to incarnate the mystery of what had happened outside the Church of the Sacred Heart on the morning of the First Communion; for we had possessed their bodies in the flesh, both living and dead.

The reconstruction at the community college was not the only spectacle to arise from Cammie and Lloyd, and linger in their wake. Another remained, and to me it was more haunting because it had slipped forever beyond our grasp. The 16mm film of the death car never, to anyone's knowledge, saw the light of day. It was packed away in a canister shaped like a single barrel of a binocular, and stored in the basement of the library. There it remained, forgotten even by Théramène, because for him at the time, film was the stuff of entertainment, and not a means of historical documentation; and in his mind, the separation was absolute. Twenty-nine years later, in the first Saturday of her appointment, a new librarian happened upon the canister, and, thinking it contained a reserve of dimes intended for the upstairs till, she opened it. She found a spoonful of brown dust. "And it did smell," she remarked later, "like a new road on a hot day." Only when she turned the canister around did she make out the faded label, penned in brown ink, "Death of the Outlaws, May 1934."

The roll of film never received so much attention in its all years of existence as upon the report of its obliteration; but perhaps there, it was only mirroring the fate of Cammie and Lloyd themselves. "What it might have told us," Théramène lamented in a letter to the *Gazette*. For by then he had come to accept, and even champion, the ascendancy of film. Indeed, Théramène had purchased the first television in town. It was delivered by van in a big, unwieldy box that could not fit through his front door, and this reminded those who were old enough of the arrival of Charpantier's bathtub, and they chuckled at the recurring instance of human folly.

"What images were etched on that roll of nitrate! What truths it might have revealed, and set forth beyond dispute!" Théramène wrote to the *Gazette*. "Do not blame me if I seem to take this matter too much to heart. I cannot help it, for I bear the name that a poet of '*le grand siècle*' assigned immortally to one who witnesses the horrific death of a son of the city, and reports on it with matchless eloquence. '*Tout son corps n'est bientot qu'une plaie*'- how my soul too reverberated with the cry, on the fateful day in May, that the bodies of our daughter Cammie Roux and our adopted son Lloyd Cannon were but a single wound! I flatter myself, not with the ability, but with the ambition, to consider and report, to bear witness and record, those events we call history with something of the eloquence of Racine's Théramène."

Ostensibly, his letter was a plea for better cataloguing in the town library, and he got around to that point by his third paragraph, but really, everyone knew the letter was his idea of a rhetorical tour de force, a musing on film, and memory, and his own first name; and it was as poetic as Théramène ever got. "Let not our own modest holdings compare to the Library of Alexandria only in ceasing to exist!" he concluded.

"He's doing well, with a line in orthodontics," my mother wrote me, with an enclosed clipping of his letter, "which is handy, as all his children have turned out as buck-toothed as jack rabbits." Théramène's letter was also the occasion for a renewed understanding between Théramène and Father Ducie, she reported. "The bodies of men indeed do wither, but the body of Holy Mother Church endures," Father Ducie said by way of greeting when he next encountered Théramène. He was clearly alluding to Théramène's missive. Théramène was so moved, briefly, that he drafted some notes towards a future article on clerics and intellectual life in early New France. But in the end, the demands of running both his dental practice and the Saint-Baptiste World History Society proved too great, and the article never advanced beyond the proposed title and a half-page outline.

The First Communion on the Wednesday in May had been surely overtaken by events. The next Sunday that the Church was free, Father Ducie performed another Communion. Once again, there were flowers, but Gabrielle's aunt was distracted by a report on the radio of a tornado off the Georgia coast when she was about to place the order, and the flowers did not arrive in time. Instead of the promised calla lilies and tea roses, we made do with baby's breath and orange blossoms left over from a wedding the day before. Poirier the baker made a batch of cake, but midway into his preparations, he found that the bottle of vanilla he'd counted on, stashed in reserve behind the flour canisters, had evaporated, and he had no more on hand. We had to settle for a mismatch of caramel frosting on a lemon-flavored cake.

"Very…Arabian," my mother said upon her first forkful, and she put down her plate. The comment depressed me, even then. It reminded me of Mrs. Nadal, and how she sought to promote her daughter's moss green dress among us, availing herself to words she'd gotten from the magazines, and through them, attempt to have us construe as elegant something that was altogether misconceived. All in all, the second First Communion had the feel of the happenstance and the substitute, of a halting re-enactment that had some of the words but lost the tune of its original. Those few children whose parents claimed they had indeed taken First Communion on the day the outlaws were shot wound up attending this second ceremony as well. Father Ducie insisted on it, and, when he alluded to his own powers of discretion over who could be confessed, confirmed, married, and buried at the Church of the Sacred Heart, the parents swallowed the air in their throats and acquiesced.

By and large, their children forsook the outfits they had worn on the Wednesday morning; and while Arlette Nadal appeared again in her lamentable moss green dress, there was no longer the shifting bank of whites and creams and ivories for it to stand out against. Perpetuée's was the only veil in sight, and the heat was so great, even by dawn, on the Sunday morning, that even she must have finally regretted the length and heft of the thing. I was in Alice-in-wonderland blue, and, for the first time outside the gleaming floorboards of my mother's house, I wore the polished white shoes. But the smell of the polish was long gone. Indeed, nothing about the day felt new or refreshed, transforming, or transformed. Instead, it felt like a dream so long forestalled that its promise had faded, and finally shimmered away.

I took Communion that day, but henceforth, I felt a secret and widening gap in my soul. It was like having a hole in my heart. It lent distinction, and potential fatality. All through the second ceremony, I was remembering the first one: how, at the moment the priest had proclaimed "*Hoc est enim corpus meum*," the officers called out, "Halt!" in bad faith, and the outlaws were shot to death, and the passage from bread and wine to the body and blood of Christ at the altar in front of us was thwarted. For certain, my life has followed in the wake of that frustration. Though this second First Communion ceremony was enacted and allowed to run its course, I believe I had already noted the disjunction between word and actuality, and that fissure was duly incorporated into my heart.

So great was the outcry among reformers in the state capitol over the charge that the officers had never given the outlaws a chance to surrender that a month later, an inquest was held. A judge-examiner was brought in from Baton Rouge. He had blond hair that scrolled over his head in stiff, even waves. Above his black and voluminous robes, his head was white and finely modelled, and, when he turned to consider first one speaker and then another, as carefully poised as a five-stringed puppet's. Every so often in the course of the two-day hearing, he waved his judgely sleeves, apropos of nothing, and they sent a cooling swish of air to those seated closest to him. He frowned seriously and took notes; he folded his brow in concentration, frequently, though not for very long.

In the end, however, he found no real fault on the part of Charpantier or his men. They left no time for the outlaws to surrender, he reasoned, but equally, the outlaws clearly had no intention of surrendering. The pistol in Lloyd's hand was entered as final proof. "They did what they had to," the report concluded; though the town eventually become confused as to whether the remark referred to the police, or to the outlaws, and by the twelfth anniversary of the event, Balthezar was quoting it in defense of Cammie and Lloyd.

Charpantier never felt vindicated because he had never felt under threat of censure, and his merry eyes and implacable belly were the same as always. Only Balthezar felt a momentary deflation because his testimony had not been requested. He lamented the evident inexperience of the magistrate; for he had sat up nights at his mother's kitchen table, making notes towards his statement and perfecting its wording. Eventually, though, these unvoiced passages took their place in his meticulously planned but unrealized memoir. Thus no effort was lost; or, more to the point, no one effort was any more lost than any other.

The day the report was released and the bulk of it reprinted in the *Gazette*, everyone in town spent the morning reading it. Claude Barbier took a table at LaFarge's and sat there for several hours, taking sips from a coffee long since gone cold, pulling a profile, and waiting to hold court with aficionados of his journalism, who never materialized. We were all too busy taking in the words of the paper themselves. So close were we to the event being recounted, that we revolved still within its orbit. I inhaled deeply of this thought along with the newsprint: if any one slight thing had been different, the slaughter would not have come to pass. For many, the death of the outlaws had about it the satisfaction of the inevitable, if not of the entirely righteous.

The report added a few details, confirmed some others, and put a few more in question. Cammie and Lloyd proceeded up the road in their car the color of desert sands. There was a rustle in the hedge of sweet mock-orange, an officer from Texas testified, and he was afraid it had alerted the outlaws to the police presence. The car moved at a steady speed towards the Church of the Sacred Heart. When it was almost directly across from the church's front step, Henderson Parker yelled "Halt," and Cammie opened her mouth to scream. Lloyd Cannon took up the wooden-handed pistol, the officers opened fire, and Father Ducie proclaimed, "This is my body." The gunfire shot all utterance to pieces. Under the barrage of firepower, Cammie and Lloyd's car slowed down, impeded. It seemed for one small moment to go almost still, but then, suddenly, vivid and unreal as a motion in a dream, it moved on. It was as if the bullets were propelling the car forward. The Texas officer testified that when he realized the car had not come to a stop but was rolling on forward, it hit him with a superstitious agony in the pit of his stomach that the outlaws were invincible to this hail of bullets; and that such a miracle had to do with the ambush being set in the shadow of the Church of the Sacred Heart.

And inside the church, the First Communicants, all in white and cream and ivory, turned away from the glittering altar laid out before their eyes. From under the opened slant of the stained glass window, there came a stirring that seemed at first like a soft spring breeze, but in reality was a burst of burned cordite from the gunfire. On the road, the wheels of the car were spewing gravel, and the tires were puncturing, and all at once, the glass of the windshield shattered. Under the sheer impact of the shots, Cammie's forearms flew up in front of her face, crossed, all a-jitter, and fell forward again. By then, Lloyd's neck had snapped backwards so that only his throat was left facing down the onslaught. There was no last look between them, Henderson Parker said.

The car rolled on, over a bump and into a tree, where its progress was finally stopped, although its motor was still running. All gunfire ceased. A second or two passed. Charpantier emerged from the leafy hedges. He rushed towards the car. He was surprisingly light on his feet for a man so heavy. A loud *halloo-oo* escaped from him. It trailed after his progress, and ascended, unfurling, into the warm spring air above us. Already, the First Communicants were poised on the blinding white steps of the church, about to swoop across the sunlit road towards the Ford car and the slaughtered outlaws, and be the first to affirm that Cammie and Lloyd were ours, and our town was a thing of substance forever.

AFTERWORD

If you enjoyed this book, you might be interested in *Judas of Memphis*.

JUDAS OF MEMPHIS
BY
E.N. MCMAHON

History records that Elvis Presley had a twin brother, Jesse, who was stillborn, and buried within hours in an unmarked grave.

But what if history is wrong? Jesse didn't die that January night in 1935, but was instead entrusted to the care of a lonely wanderer - a man who, stumbling into Depression-era Mississippi, embraced it as a second promised land. Studded with the names of his childhood - Jericho, Cairo, Bethlehem, and Memphis - it is a land steeped in belief, a land which offers him a new hope to replace the one he lost all those years ago, when he was forced to consign his own brother to the cross. Perhaps, after all his years of exile, Judas Iscariot - Jesus's twin brother - has finally been given a second chance....

Judas of Memphis is a story of faith, fate, and redemption, of sibling rivalry and paternal love, and a bold re-imagining of familiar legends both ancient and American

ABOUT THE AUTHOR

E N McMahon has a Master's degree from the London School of Economics, and a PhD in French literature from Duke University. She has worked as a reporter, television researcher, bagel maker (briefly), and (even more briefly) in encyclopedia sales. She divides her time between England and America.

www.ingramcontent.com/pod-product-compliance
Lightning Source LLC
Chambersburg PA
CBHW022131170626
46808CB00002B/944